JENNIFER S. ALDERSON

Forgeries and Fatalities

First published by Traveling Life Press 2024

Copyright © 2024 by Jennifer S. Alderson

All rights reserved. No part of this publication may be reproduced, stored or transmitted in any form or by any means, electronic, mechanical, photocopying, recording, scanning, or otherwise without written permission from the publisher. It is illegal to copy this book, post it to a website, or distribute it by any other means without permission.

This novel is entirely a work of fiction. The names, characters and incidents portrayed in it are the work of the author's imagination. Any resemblance to actual persons, living or dead, events or localities is entirely coincidental.

Jennifer S. Alderson asserts the moral right to be identified as the author of this work.

First edition

ISBN: 9789083169767

This book was professionally typeset on Reedsy. Find out more at reedsy.com

Contents

1	Not One Of Us	1
2	Lady Sophie to the Rescue	8
3	We Meet Again	16
4	A True Artist	26
5	Question Time	31
6	An Indecent Proposal	37
7	Myrtle Sends an Update	42
8	Hold Your Horses	45
9	Round One	49
10	Up the Ante	58
11	Eyes of a Dragonfly	61
12	The Diva Arrives	69
13	Second Round of Bidding	73
14	The Winner Is	81
15	From Father to Son	89
16	So Many Possibilities	96
17	There Goes My Lead	101
18	Shipping Snafu	106
19	A Flight To Venice	110
20	Leaving on a Jet Plane	116
21	Family Reunion	124
22	Oddly Evasive	130
23	Forced Into Retirement	137
24	Sleeping In	141
25	The Texans Come Clean	145
26	The Arrival	148

27	No Discretion	156
28	Tiaras and Film Stars	160
29	Romance in the Air	165
30	Catching Dave Up	168
31	Guns Blazing	172
32	To Kill or Not To Kill	177
33	Murderer on the Loose	179
34	Police Station Espresso	184
35	A Sunny Day in Venice	187
36	Meeting Esmerelda	191
37	Interagency Cooperation	195
Acknowledgements		198
About the Author		199
Death on the Danube: A New Year's Murder in Budapest		201
The Lover's Portrait: An Art Mystery		204

1

Not One Of Us

"Who let you in?" Cyril Bouve—the host of this evening's exclusive event—cried out, indignation coloring his voice.

The squat man was so upset that his entire body was trembling. It was easy to see thanks to his loose-fitting tunic and the long silk scarf he wore, presumably to help hide his bulging torso. A small diamond stud was half-hidden in a fold in his left ear, and a thick gold chain circled his even thicker neck. His clothing style and body shape reminded me of Marlon Brando in his later years. Unfortunately, Cyril was not as carefree as the vibe his costume exuded.

His party planner, a spindly young woman named Margreta who towered over him, was already at his side. "Ms. Rhodes is here at the bequest of Lady Sophie Rutherford, sir."

Cyril glowered up at Rhonda Rhodes, my best friend and the reason I was able to get into this private auction of paintings created by our host. "I cannot believe that Lady Sophie is acquainted with someone as uncultured as you!"

I gazed up at the ceiling, wondering how this assignment had gone wrong so quickly. Maybe I had been too optimistic about Rhonda's abilities to take my partner's place. While she did not have the social connections that Sophie did, Rhonda had celebrity status as the presenter of the incredibly popular television show, *Antiques Time*. During our last impromptu assignment, that connection alone had helped me to recover a collection of expensive movie props and catch a killer.

Yet her charms seemed to go unnoticed by Cyril Bouve, ex-con and current owner of The Bouve Gallery. I had expected that he—a convicted forger who now sold copies of famous paintings for a living—and Rhonda—an appraiser known for being able to eyeball estimate pretty much anything thanks to her extensive knowledge of the art world—would bond over their mutual appreciation of a wide range of artists.

But no, Cyril apparently fancied himself a real artist, or at least imagined himself to be on a higher social plane than my oh-so-charming bestie.

His snobbery was even suspicious seeing as I was here to follow up on a trustworthy tip linking Cyril to a long-active art smuggling operation, one with its tentacles spread across Europe. The nature of his involvement was far from clear. Nor was I one hundred percent certain that our informant hadn't made a wrong assumption about what they'd seen. As a senior art sleuth for the Rosewood Agency, a private organization specializing in art recovery, I was tasked with finding out.

That was why Rhonda and I were in this lounge, deep inside of Luxembourg's High Security Hub, waiting to view the art that Cyril was selling off tonight. Figuring out why the annual auction was being held inside of this free port—a tax-free zone for goods in transit, situated next to Luxembourg Airport—instead of an Italian gallery, as usual, was another puzzle for me to solve.

When we'd entered the building, the stark concrete foyer reminded me of an evil lair fit for a James Bond film. Yet the private showrooms, available for use by the free port's clients, were tastefully decorated with extensive wooden paneling and a flowery wallpaper that would make anyone above sixty feel right at home.

Seeing as my usual partner—Baroness Sophie Rutherford, or the Baroness for short—was lying in a hospital with a fractured foot, Rhonda had graciously flown over to take her place. On my own, I simply wasn't interesting enough to be admitted to these sorts of affairs. Yet, if I couldn't quickly convince our host that Rhonda was not an uncouth buffoon, we would soon be ejected from this fancy shindig. If only my bestie had taken a better look at that coat rack, we wouldn't be in this mess.

The evening had started off on a high note when Josie and Johnny Bighorn, a lovely couple from Texas, proved to be fans of Rhonda's show. We'd been having a good chat, until Rhonda's bag began to pull on her shoulder. Instead of setting it down on the floor next to her, she'd spotted a treelike structure in the corner and hung her bag on one of the branches. Her purse couldn't have weighed that much, but it was enough to snap off one side of the thing. Unfortunately for Rhonda, it was not a coat rack, but an expensive work of art.

"There's no reason to panic. I'm happy to pay for the restoration, or for the purchase of a new one."

"Are you certain you can afford to?" our host snapped. "It's a geometric sculpture by Kylie, and it tripled in value last year because she died in a freak manufacturing accident. I can't just order a new one. If the free port sends me a bill for it, I'm forwarding it on to you."

Instead of being mortified, Rhonda guffawed. "Well, we'd better find ourselves a hot glue gun or some duct tape. I usually carry a roll with me, but this purse is too small."

When she pulled her hand back to slap our host amicably on the shoulder, I caught her arm and held it tight instead, knowing he would not appreciate being on the receiving end of such an intimate gesture from her.

Cyril removed his round, John Lennon-style glasses and began to clean them with such intensity I was afraid the glass would crack. The action must have calmed him down because when he replaced the eyepiece, his voice was far more steady. "I must insist that you leave."

"Wait a second—you can't kick her out. Don't you know who this is—it's Rhonda Rhodes!" Josie Bighorn exclaimed, her many rhinestone armbands jangling together as she pointed her finger at my friend. She and her rancher husband had clearly taken a shine to my friend, which had been a great relief to both of us.

Before we had arrived, I had assumed that Rhonda's exuberant personality would make it easy for us to get close to the other invitees. She'd certainly used her natural charisma to win over the guests at the last party we'd attended. If I was going to work out who else may be involved in this smuggling operation, I needed to converse with—or eavesdrop on—as many of the guests as possible, in the hopes of picking up a few clues as to what was really going on. Yet most of the invitees were minor royals who seemed immune to her folksy charm and completely uninterested in her television show.

Unfortunately, our host had not yet warmed up to her, either. "Yes, she's the host of that awful *Antiques Time*. I am happy to say that I have not seen any of her shows. Television is drivel for lazy minds and not worth my time."

I puffed out my cheeks, wondering what to do next. I had clearly overestimated Rhonda's ability to blend in here. The mission was more important than standing up for my friend, yes, but I figured that if she was kicked out, I would be, too. I was her plus-one, after all. Before I could think up an appropriately restrained rebuttal, the Westworths—another of the *nouveau riche* couples in attendance that Rhonda and I had briefly conversed with earlier—chimed in.

"Come on, Cyril. You put up with the likes of me and Trish. Why can't you stand Rhonda?" His English accent was so thick, I had trouble understanding him.

I'd already noticed that Trish and Gary Westworth had been chuckling over their beers as they watched Rhonda and Cyril argue, apparently enjoying the show. Thanks to their shiny, sharkskin-like suits, they were hard to miss.

Earlier, I had wondered why these two had been invited. During the preceding cocktail hour, the English couple had been relentlessly poking fun at our host and several of the posher guests. It was only after Trish informed Rhonda that they regularly purchased Cyril's reproductions in bulk and used them to decorate the cabins of their cruise ships that I understood why they were always invited to his auctions and gallery shows.

I'd never cruised before, but did recognize the name of their company as one of the most popular and luxurious cruise ship operators in Europe. Which explained why the other guests didn't bite back at Gary's nastier remarks. I figured they must be worried about possibly being blacklisted from booking a cruise with his company, if they did.

Which was why Gary apparently felt comfortable enough to egg our host on.

Cyril narrowed his eyes at the Englishman. "Because you and I have a past, Gary. I want nothing to do with this one. Margreta, are you certain Lady Sophie wanted this person to have her invitation?" After taking a long look at Rhonda, he added, "Especially one dressed like that."

I had to admit, we were horribly underdressed for the occasion, which was my fault—not Rhonda's. I should have persuaded her to wear something more subtle. Our fellow female invitees were wearing the newest creations from Coco Chanel, Christian Dior, and Vera Wang, as well as enough jewelry to make most of them sparkle more than the chandeliers lighting up the tastefully decorated space.

Rhonda's lime-green jacket over an electric-blue dress clashed horribly with their haute couture. Her pink glasses rimmed with fake diamonds completed the blinding outfit, yet didn't help matters. I figured her role as a television personality would give her license to be different, and it was what she felt most comfortable in. But I should have known better. My own choice wasn't that great, either. My navy pantsuit was mighty boring in comparison to Rhonda's outfit. Yet even topped with a tailored black jacket and silk Hermès scarf, it wasn't nearly fancy enough for the occasion.

Of the forty or so guests present, the Texan and English couples were the only other ones who had dared to dress differently than the rest. Perhaps that was why they'd been open to standing up for Rhonda. Unfortunately, I feared neither couple would be able to get us out of this mess.

Cyril's assistant also unashamedly examined Rhonda's costume, her lips pursed in the same fashion as her boss's. "Yes, sir; last week her ladyship informed me of her injuries and asked us to extend Rhonda Rhodes the same courtesy we had her. I had no idea who Rhodes was, sir."

I had to pinch my hand to keep myself from protesting aloud. When we'd arrived at the party, she'd squealed in delight, then babbled about how jealous her mom was going to be, before begging Rhonda to take several selfies with her.

Cyril looked around the room, as if he was searching for a security guard, before announcing, "Can someone please escort this person out of my space?"

I wanted to scream in frustration. All of the favors my partner had needed to call in were about to be for naught. Not only was my boss, Reginald Pinky Rosewood—Reggie, for short—going to be livid, Sophie would probably remind me that she'd told me so. In contrast to my employer, she was convinced that Rhonda was the wrong person to fill her shoes at this party. Right now, I would give anything to have the Baroness by my side. But I knew she needed to remain flat on her back, until her injuries healed.

I stepped in between Cyril and Rhonda, ignoring the party planner completely. "This is all a horrible misunderstanding. Baroness Rutherford extended Ms. Rhodes her invitation after she was injured, so that Ms. Rhodes could bid on several paintings for her. If you exclude her from this auction, you are in fact excluding Lady Sophie."

Cyril crossed his arms over his ample torso and tapped his fingers on his tunic's sleeve. "No, that is not correct. I would welcome Lady Sophie with open arms. She may not be a client, but is a friend. This person, however..." He raised an eyebrow as he took in Rhonda's bright outfit one more time. "...could never take her ladyship's place. Now if you will excuse me, you have wasted enough of my time. Margreta, get them out of here before the others begin to gossip."

The irritating little man whipped his scarf around his neck before turning on his heel and walking away. My heart sank; we hadn't even seen the artwork yet, let alone gotten to know the guests better. And there was no way we would be able to sneak back into the party later, because this building was a heavily guarded fortress.

Rhonda must have sensed my frustration. Although she didn't know all of my reasons for being here, she was aware that my objective was to study the artwork Bouve had on offer. She knew as well as I did that if we got kicked out now, it would be another year before we had a chance to get this close to his operation. Which was why, I had to assume, that she chose to try another tactic.

When she started after Cyril, the glint in her eye made my stomach knot up. Yet she was faster and caught up with him before I could stop her. "I sure am sorry to hear you think I'm not good enough to be at your little party."

Her tone was more perturbed than offended. From what she'd told me about her many interactions with fans, most of the people who recognized her on the street were kind individuals who were simply pleased to briefly meet her. Yet there were always a few sad souls who found it necessary to try to upset her by denigrating what she did for a living. Which was probably why she already had a retort ready to go.

"Say, don't you make copies of real artwork? Those sound like collectibles to me. I wonder if I've ever had any of your work on my show—I'll have to ask my producer about it. Wouldn't that be a kick?"

Although I had to applaud her quick comeback, this was definitely not the right moment to antagonize him.

"I do not make reproductions—mine are real works of art! That's why my forgeries fooled those supposed experts for years. My paintings are exact copies of the originals and utterly indistinguishable from them. Which is why I call them repeats, not replicas." Our host screeched so loudly that if the room wasn't soundproof, we would soon have a security team breaking down the door.

"Now get out—you are not welcome here!"

2

Lady Sophie to the Rescue

When Cyril pointed to the door, my heart sank in the knowledge that we had royally messed up this important assignment. Both my partner and boss were going to be livid when they heard what had happened.

Before I could figure out how to salvage this situation, a soft cough made us all turn towards the doorway. Sitting in a wheelchair, with her bandaged foot raised up in front of her, was my partner, Lady Sophie Rutherford. A rather matronly looking older woman with her gaze averted downwards stood behind the chair, her hands clenched around the handles.

I almost ran over and planted a kiss on my partner's cheek, before recalling that she hated public displays of affection. Besides, it would be unusual for a personal assistant to kiss her boss, no matter the circumstances.

"Lady Sophie!" Rhonda squealed before curtsying in front of my injured partner. "What are you doing here? Aren't you supposed to be in the hospital, recuperating?"

I was wondering the same thing, but knew better than to ask Sophie such a personal question in such a public way. I studied her face critically, glad to see the swelling in her jaw was gone and the bruising could now be hidden under a thick layer of makeup. Her emerald ballgown and canary diamond necklace did help to brighten up her appearance. Her nurse's salmon-colored frock and garish makeup, however, did nothing to liven up the woman's sallow complexion. I wondered briefly where Sophie had found her, but wasn't about to ask.

My partner narrowed her eyes at my bestie—her expression making quite clear that she was here to clean up our mess, not chitchat—before stretching her arms out to our host. When she did, the plethora of diamonds embedded in Sophie's tiara caught the light, illuminating her head like a halo.

"Dear Cyril, please do forgive my American acquaintance. She may be a touch uncouth, but she is an avid collector and a good person, despite that bling-bling façade." Apparently her jaw hadn't quite healed because Sophie gritted her teeth as she spoke, as if it hurt to do so.

"She is a television celebrity, after all," the Baroness added in a loud whisper audible to all, as if that explained everything.

Apparently, to Cyril, it did. "Of course," he murmured in Rhonda's direction, before grasping the Baroness's hands and pulling them close. "Lady Sophie, it is an honor to have you grace us with your presence tonight, especially considering your injuries."

Sophie batted her eyelashes and looked away demurely as he bent down to kiss her knuckles. I felt like I was watching a scene from *Gone with the Wind*; all that Sophie needed was a fan to wave in front of her.

Our host glared at Rhonda again, yet let her be, choosing to engage the Baroness in conversation instead. The way he turned his back to us made clear that we were not to take part.

"Let's get away from Cyril and mingle with the others before he changes his mind," I whispered into Rhonda's ear as I pulled her farther into the room. It was a rather small space, filled with high tables for drinks but few chairs. A freestanding bar was placed on one side of the room, and a bartender stood behind, at the ready.

"Boy, that man really gets under your skin," Rhonda huffed, thankfully after we were out of Cyril's earshot.

I turned towards a waiter holding a tray of champagne and grabbed two glasses. As uncouth as it was, I downed half of one before handing the other to Rhonda.

"Don't worry about Cyril, he doesn't matter," I fibbed, as the champagne bubbles tickled my throat. "You were a hit at the last party, and you're going to kill it tonight, too."

Rhonda sucked in her breath. "Please don't use that expression ever again. After that pirate party, it hits too close to home."

"Fair enough. They are going to love you. Now, shall we try mingling again?"

Rhonda looked around the room, apparently taking in the many guests circling about. "Sure thing. Who should we chat up first?"

Unfortunately, after the coat rack incident and Cyril's dressing down, several guests literally gave us the cold shoulder by turning away from us when we approached. But the night was still young, and from what I'd overheard the party planner tell her boss, less than half of the invitees were present. I assumed the auction would only commence once more guests had arrived, meaning I still had time to eavesdrop on his guests' conversations before we viewed the art, even if they refused to converse with us.

The evidence our informant had passed on about Cyril's supposedly illicit activities was perhaps a little flimsy, but given the fact that the artist specialized in creating exact copies of missing artwork, it was worth checking out. Even though we did not know whether any of the invitees might be working with him, my boss and I did assume that if he had an accomplice, that person would be present tonight.

I scanned the room, assessing each guest's potential as Cyril's partner in this possibly fictitious scheme. Several minor royals were grouped together and chatting loudly. But that crowd seemed to be more interested in one-upping each other about their recent vacations and expensive purchases than in discussing Cyril's artwork.

One nervous-looking man wearing a particularly well-tailored tuxedo spoke quietly into his phone, yet loudly enough to allow me to work out that he was Russian. A quick look at his phone's screen as I passed him by—open to stock market updates—told me the conversation was probably about his investment portfolio and not Cyril's work.

A few feet away, an elderly couple were trying to wheedle the ingredients of a particular *hors d'oeuvre* out of a confused-looking waiter. The young man looked as if he badly wanted to escape the conversation, yet did not know how to do so in a polite fashion. The burr in the couple's voices also betrayed their nationality, in this case, Scottish.

My eyes swept the room once again, until I homed in on three groups of business types standing on the other side. A quartet of thick-necked Italians huddled in a far corner, seemingly all talking simultaneously. Another group of five Asian businessmen congregated around one table, while a trio of Spanish investors stood clustered around another.

If I'd had to venture a guess, I would have said they were representatives of three different investment firms, here to bid on artwork for their clients or company. It wasn't simply because they showed no interest in mingling with the others. What really gave them away for me was the blandness of their suits. In comparison to the rest, they were wearing rather boring, off-the-rack designs with no further embellishments. They weren't here to be seen or make a social splash, as many of the other guests obviously were. They were here for business.

I considered again who to approach first, even though it felt a bit pointless at the moment. Until I could see and hear how Cyril interacted with his guests, there was no real way of knowing who he might be working with. Up until the coat rack incident, Cyril had flitted from conversation to conversation with little more than a quick hello, before setting off again. I only hoped he would spend more time talking with his invitees once the viewing and auction got underway.

I tried to catch Sophie's eye, wondering whether she had any candidates in mind. But she was too engrossed in her conversation with Cyril and a small group of well-dressed guests to notice. Besides, with Rhonda by my side, I couldn't really have a candid chat with her. My bestie had done nothing but antagonize our host since we had arrived, and I wouldn't be surprised if Cyril was still searching for an excuse to have us removed from the premises, despite Sophie's presence. I couldn't risk her saying something gauche again before I had the chance to examine the artwork he was auctioning off.

So I turned back to Rhonda. "Why don't we start with that group of Spanish speakers, on your right."

Yet before we could make our move, the Texans were back and blocking our path. They were the first couple I'd steered us towards after we'd arrived, simply because of Josie's outfit. The Texan wore a babydoll dress and jacket similar to Rhonda's, yet in even brighter shades than my friend's ensemble.

Her husband, Johnny, was dressed in a tuxedo that could only have been made in the Deep South. The front and back were decorated with extensive scroll work, and the sleeves were embedded with rhinestones that reflected the light every time he moved. His ten-gallon hat had a brim so wide, his eyes were permanently in the shadows.

"Cyril sure is in a bad mood tonight. I don't know what got into him, but he had no right to talk to you like that," Johnny declared.

"I suppose, but I should have known that the tree thingy was a sculpture, and not a coat rack." Rhonda looked to the floor, as if she was unable to meet the Texans' eyes.

Josie pooh-pooh'ed away that thought with a flick of her wrist. "Don't mind him. It does looks just like a fancy hall tree, and it was placed in the corner—what did the interior designer expect people to think?"

"Cyril's probably taking his frustration out on you, that's all," Johnny added. "Maybe it's because so few guests bothered to show up. Holding the auction in this dreary spot by the airport didn't make it enticing enough for most guests, I bet. The last few he'd hosted were held in Venice. Besides that, he usually announces these auctions months in advance, but for this one he only sent out the invitations a few weeks ago. From what I'd heard from a few of the other guests, it sounds like Cyril was having trouble getting everything done in time for this show."

I nodded, as if in sympathy, but really I was agreeing with him. This party had almost slipped under our radar, as well, but thanks to an alert friend of Reggie's, the Rosewood Agency had learned about this pop-up auction soon after the first invitations went out.

"But Cyril has always had a short fuse, so I'm certain he would have found something to be upset about," Josie added.

"True. That's why I wouldn't have flown over here just for this auction. But my little lady and I were already in Europe on a shopping spree, so it was easy to fit it in."

I coughed into my hand, to stop myself from giggling. There was nothing little about Josie Bighorn. It wasn't just that she had a Rubenesque-body shape; the shoulder pads on her florescent-yellow jacket jutted out so far they made her look like a linebacker, and her hair was so bouffant that I wondered whether she had to turn to the side, just to walk through a doorway.

"How long are you planning on being here in Europe?" Rhonda asked. "I just flew over to do some sightseeing with Carmen. We've been talking about visiting the French Riviera and Prague next, but haven't booked any flights yet. Although Trish has got me thinking about going on one of their shorter cruises before I have to fly back. They sure do sound luxurious! I could do with a little more pampering before we start shooting *Antiques Time* again."

"Oh, they are, honey. We took their twelve-city Mediterranean cruise last year and loved it. You two really should go on one, even if it's only for a few days. I haven't felt so relaxed in ages." Josie turned to her husband. "Do you think we'll have time to take a short one, while we're over here?"

Johnny ran a hand over his chin, considering. "We do have a long list to get through, but I'm sure we can make the time."

"Oh, Johnny!" Josie gave her man a smooch so passionate, it made me blush.

"What are you two shopping for?" I asked while keeping my eyes averted, hoping my question would force the two lovebirds to pull out of their amorous embrace. I wasn't a complete prude, but did have trouble with extreme public displays of affection, such as this. I never knew where to point my gaze.

The two pulled apart, and Josie turned to answer me, as if nothing unusual had happened. "We're buying furniture and artwork for Johnny's new office. Instead of paying top dollar for the old masters or antiques, we're looking at investing in contemporary European artists and designers this time around. It's fascinating to see the new trends in design, but I'm not sure about the art yet. I am more of a fan of realism than abstract works. Up until tonight, that's all we've been seeing."

Rhonda nodded. "I am with you on that. Whenever someone brings an abstract piece onto my show, I always check to make sure they are holding it the right way up, before I make my analysis. Sometimes it's hard to tell!"

Johnny chortled. "I just read about a Mondrian painting that has been hanging upside down in a German museum for years. An art historian only figured it out a few weeks ago, when she found an old photograph of Mondrian working on the piece in his studio."

Rhonda sniggered. "Oh, my! How embarrassing. Did they rehang it?"

Josie leaned forward and laid a hand on her arm, setting her bracelets jangling again. "No, they did not. The museum decided to leave it as it is, because that's how their visitors have experienced it for the past five decades. Can you believe it?"

When the three began to laugh riotously, garnering a few dirty looks from the conservative guests standing close, I knew Rhonda was in good hands. So I gave her a slight nod, signaling that I was going to mingle with the others.

As much as I loved having her here by my side, it was frustrating not being able to talk shop with her. She'd been briefed about why I wanted to go to this party—to help flush out an art smuggling ring—but I had been ordered by my boss to not tell her the entire truth about my current assignment. Which was why she thought I was here writing an investigative piece for *Hidden Treasures*, a magazine dedicated to antiques and collectibles. The publication did exist, but all of the articles bearing my byline were ghostwritten by a professional.

For that reason, a huge part of me was glad that my real partner, Lady Sophie Rutherford, had unexpectedly shown up when she did. Not only did she manage to get us un-ejected, but also I could rely on her to contact Rosewood and let them know what had happened if things went sideways again. Although I did hope that her stubborn refusal to remain in bed and rest her foot would not have lasting consequences for her future ability to waltz or tango.

Yet as much as I wanted to pull Sophie aside and talk this case through, doing so while she was interacting with our host would not be a smart move. That meant it was time for me to switch from eavesdropping, to interrogation mode. The investors interested me the most, so I decided to start with the group closest to me. I tousled my long hair and put on my biggest grin, hoping they were heterosexual and up for a chat.

As I began to cross over to them, though, a vaguely familiar voice rose up from behind, his words sending a shiver up my spine. "Carmen De Luca—what are you doing here?"

3

We Meet Again

"I didn't expect to see you at this party. Are you Baroness Rutherford's plus-one again?"

My eyes widened as I turned to face the speaker, hoping all the while that I had misplaced his voice. I wasn't used to being recognized at these events simply because the guest lists tended to vary wildly, depending on the host's personality. Also my role as either an antiques journalist or the Baroness's personal assistant meant I tended to be ignored by most of the wealthy and important guests. Which was lucky for me. When I first started out, I had tried to wear disguises, but wigs tended to pop off of my unruly hair at the most inopportune moments.

When I turned to face the speaker, my heart sank further. Unfortunately, he was the person I had feared would be standing behind me. I kept that smile plastered on, but toned it down a notch. "Dave, right? Didn't we meet a month ago, at the Moreaus' villa in France?"

That part was true. Harold Moreau's party had been the first assignment for me and the Baroness on this Europe tour. I did recall meeting him there, not only because he was good-looking, but also because he did not fit the typical profile of a wealthy patron of the arts.

Dave had claimed to have wanted to bid on one of Harold's rare illuminated manuscripts, even though he didn't appear to know much about them. Not that a lack of knowledge had stopped many wealthy collectors from buying art they knew nothing about. Yet, in contrast to the rest of the guests, he had worn an off-the-rack suit and very little jewelry, making me wonder whether he could have even have afforded to purchase any of Harold's million-dollar books.

And yet here he was, attending this extremely exclusive auction that even the Baroness—a favorite of socialites—had difficulty securing a ticket to. So who was he to warrant an invitation?

As much as I wanted to find out what Dave's backstory was and ask how he'd gotten into this party, the last time I'd seen him, I had been masquerading as a reporter for *Hidden Treasures*. I hoped he would be smart enough to keep his mouth shut about my fake profession, at least around the host and his party planner. I didn't know how Cyril would react to having a member of the press here—even a lowly freelancer writing for an antiques-based periodical—if he was involved in something illicit. But I would rather not find out.

"Yes, I'm here as a guest of the Baroness," I said. Technically that was true; Rhonda and I had used Sophie's invitation to get inside.

He smirked but didn't blow my cover, at least not yet. "What happened to Lady Sophie? I saw her roll in earlier. Did she have an accident or surgery?"

"I'm afraid it was an accident. A Ming vase fell on her foot, and both shattered." Technically, that was the truth, but Dave didn't need to know all of the details. The Baroness had fractured her foot while saving my life—I owed her big-time for that one.

"That sounds horrible. It's good she could make it to the party, regardless. It should be an interesting night."

His comment made my forehead crease. "What do you mean, an interesting night?"

Yet before he could answer, a thin and terribly fashion-conscious older man rushed up to Dave. "Mr. Swanson, where is your lovely companion? I seem to have lost sight of her."

When he glanced over at me, he added, "No offense to you, my beauty."

The finely dressed Italian's voice was so melodious, it was almost musical. Yet the man looked at me with such a lecherous grin, I couldn't help but grimace.

"She had to bow out, I'm afraid; the salmon pâté didn't agree with her."

His comment about his sickly companion reminded me of a female partygoer I'd seen exiting just minutes after Rhonda and I had arrived. It had struck me as odd that anyone would be leaving so soon. The young lady had her back to me the entire time, but there was something about the way she moved that reminded me of Julie, Rhonda's oldest daughter. Not that any embassy administrative assistants would have been invited to a fancy party like this.

Still, I had been drawn to the young woman, but she had left before I could get close to her. Considering how much trouble it had been to get inside this place, I certainly wasn't going to leave and risk not getting let back in. Besides, I imagined it would have scared the poor girl to death, if I had raced up to her and asked to take a better look at her face.

The Italian leaned back on his heel and held a hand to his heart, as if he had been shot. "I must tell our host to never use that caterer again! It is a shame she had to leave; I was looking forward to getting to know her better."

Instead of being offended that the randy older man was speaking in that way about his companion, Dave smiled back in a similarly lewd manner. "I'm certain she would have enjoyed that. Perhaps another time."

The man bowed and clicked the heels of his Hermès loafers together as he winked at me, before leaving us alone again.

"Is your friend really ill, or was that just an excuse to get away from that creep? Who is that guy anyway?" I mumbled, hopefully softly enough that none of the other guests could hear.

"No, something didn't agree with her, and she left the party shortly after we arrived. And that creep, as you aptly put it, is Nico Manzino. He's an Italian gallery owner who works with Cyril on these annual auctions."

Dave took a long sip of his drink, effectively cutting off our conversation, and began to look around, as if he was searching the room for someone.

As hot as he is, he sure can be rude, I thought. It was always hard not to feel insulted when a guest cold-shouldered me at a party. But then again, I was nothing more than the plus-one of someone interesting and rich.

I was about to walk away from him, when Dave's eyebrows suddenly shot up and his attention seemed to focus on something or someone behind me. I turned to follow his line of sight and ended up staring straight at Cyril. Dave's eyes narrowed as he took in our host, standing alone for the first time tonight.

Cyril, however, pretended that he didn't notice that we were both focused on him.

"If you'll excuse me…" Dave strode off without another glance.

However, before Dave reached our host, the lecherous Italian caught up with Cyril. The artist reared back, as if he was offended by Nico's intrusion of his personal space. When he tried to sidestep the art dealer, in a clear attempt at avoiding the man, I knew I needed to get closer and find out why.

The Italian blocked his path and said something to Cyril before I could cross the room. Dave also seemed to be heading in their direction, but stopped and frowned at me when he noted how close I already was to the pair.

Just as I was near enough to understand them, Cyril tried to rush off again, but Manzino grabbed onto his arm and held on tight.

"I told you we would talk after the auction. It's time to view the art, even if so many of the guests are fashionably late," Cyril hissed as he tugged on his captive arm, pulling it loose from the Italian's grip on the second try.

When Manzino began to protest, Cyril ignored him, and clinked his wristwatch against his glass. The sharp clanking noise had the rest looking to him expectantly.

"If I can please have your attention, it is time to view my latest creations."

As the murmur in the room intensified, I could feel the anticipation amongst the guests rising. His repeats were copies of lost artwork, which was a fascinating gimmick, I could give him that. But they were copies, nonetheless. I was certain that part of the attraction was simply the fact that Cyril Bouve was one of the world's most famous contemporary artists working today.

Yet his fame had more to do with his checkered past and illicit activities than with the artwork that he currently peddled. In the span of twenty years,

Cyril had forged hundreds of prints, etchings, and paintings so true to the originals that they had fooled almost every specialist in the museum world. Once a few of Cyril's works had been discovered to be fakes, it had taken the FBI, CIA, Interpol, and a whole bunch of other organizations several years to finally catch the guy.

At his trial, Cyril had used the witness stand as a podium to present his reasons for forging the art. He maintained that it was to prove that most art experts were charlatans who couldn't tell a fake from the works they professed to know intimately. If they had possessed that ability, he asserted, they would have spotted his fraudulent work immediately.

He'd made such an intelligent impression on the press and jury that he'd gotten off with little more than a slap on the wrist. A TV series about his life and trial, as well as a six-figure book deal that hinged on the manuscript being finished before he was released from prison, turned him into a loveable rogue and the media's darling.

The day of his release, his autobiography hit the bestseller lists in twenty-four countries. The fact that he was free to go, despite having refused to provide the authorities with a complete list of all of the artwork he had forged, only added to the mystique surrounding his persona.

Cyril had shown no remorse or shame for his actions, upon his release or since. Instead, he immediately reinvented himself as the world's best painter of "repeats"—paintings so true to the original that a specialist would have trouble determining which was the copy and which was the real deal. To keep himself out of prison, he boldly scrawled his signature across the front and back of each painting.

At first his new business model didn't garner much interest, until he began re-creating masterpieces that had been destroyed during World War II. That was how he'd gained the reputation of being able to bring "lost" art back to life. Once his concept caught on, he migrated to selling more commissions than prepainted artwork. From what I'd gathered from his website, his gallery was primarily filled with oils that weren't for sale, but served as examples of what he was capable of. Most could also be purchased in bulk as lithographs.

As an ode to his gallery's origins, he held this special "Lost Masterpieces" action once a year. These days, he ran one gallery in Luxembourg City and sold his repeats in several more galleries dotted around Europe. From what I had understood from the party planner and the Texans, this was the first time that he'd held this auction here in this free port, instead of in Manzino's gallery in Venice, Italy. Whether it had to do with Cyril being behind schedule or for a more dubious reason, I could not yet say.

When Cyril opened an unmarked door at the back of the space, the clicking noise snapped me back to reality and my current assignment. Our host led us down a narrow hallway and past a gender-neutral restroom, before turning to the right a few feet later. Before him was another door, this one fitted with a keypad.

Drat, there goes my chance! I felt like an amateur, knowing I should have pushed my way to the front, in case of a situation such as this, instead of hanging back so I could speak to Sophie before we both entered the gallery. When I noticed the security device, I tried to jostle my way forward while ensuring my torso was aimed at Cyril's fingers. But it was no good; I was too slow, and other guests got in the way of the pinhole camera attached to my brooch.

Which meant I was out of luck. The new infrared filter I'd installed on my phone—a special filter that enabled me to see which keys Cyril had pushed in thanks to their thermal registration—only worked if the pictures were taken within a few seconds of the user pressing on the pad.

After the last party, when my telephone had been taken from me by the host, I'd had a hankering to buy new pieces of surveillance gear. As soon as I'd returned to Amsterdam, I picked up a few gadgets and a tiny burner phone. My favorite purchase was the brooch currently attached to my pantsuit—a gorgeous dragonfly pin that a security expert had fitted with a camera, its video feed automatically saved to the cloud and accessible from my phone.

Johnny's wide-brimmed hat certainly had not helped my view, especially considering he had already pushed his way to the front of the pack. When the gallery door clicked open, the Texan made a point of standing on his toes and looking back at the guests clustered together behind him.

"Well, I'll be. Josie, we might stand a chance at winning a bid this time—I don't see Serena De Ville."

"Wouldn't that be a stroke of luck, if she didn't show," his wife added, pleasure emanating from her voice. "She outbid us on every piece I wanted last time."

Cyril chuckled. "I am sorry to disappoint you, but I do expect to see her later. She's just fashionably late, as usual." His comment was meant to be light, but I sensed some underlying irritation, presumably with his tardy guest.

He cleared his throat, yet held his hand on the doorknob, waiting until he had everyone's attention. "As you all know, literally thousands of masterworks were lost during the Second World War and its aftermath. Which is why I have channeled my extensive skills into bringing these masterworks back to life, so the world can enjoy them again."

When several guests began to applaud, I bit on my tongue to stop myself from saying something nasty. *Wow, he is not short on self-confidence*, I thought. Which was surprising, given his upbringing. Watching him, one would never guess that Cyril was really the son of a traveling salesman and one of eight mouths to feed. It had taken Myrtle and her co-workers at the Rosewood Agency a lot of digging to find that out. Maybe, having never had money when he was a kid, he was making up for it now. Whatever the reason, I found it fascinating to watch him work. However, my bestie did not seem to agree.

"What a pompous little…" I heard Rhonda muttering behind me, which is why I planted the thick heel of my Louis Vuitton slingback pump firmly onto her toes. If I'd been wearing stilettos, I would have elbowed her, instead. The tiny yelp confirmed that I had hit my target, and her resulting silence established that she'd understood my message.

Only after the applause died out did Cyril announce, "I give you this year's lost masterpieces."

He opened the door with a flourish and stood back, allowing his guests to rush through. When they began elbowing each other to get inside, I walked to the back of the group where my wheelchair-bound partner and her nurse were waiting, figuring this might be my only chance to speak with Sophie this evening.

Her nurse's eyes widened to saucers when she noticed me approaching fast, and I swore her hands began to tremble. *The poor thing must be completely out of her element*, I realized.

I nodded to the frightened-looking woman before leaning down until my mouth was at my partner's ear level.

"What are you doing here, Sophie? You are supposed to keep weight off your foot for at least four weeks. It's only been ten days," I whispered through a smile, hoping my use of her first name would signal how seriously angry I was that she had disobeyed her doctor's orders and come to the party.

"It's good to see you, too," she said, her sarcasm not lost on me. When she jerked her head up to glare at me, I could see from the dilation of her pupils that she was high on painkillers.

"As long as I remain seated, my doctor gave me the okay to be here. That is why I have this nurse with me to ensure I don't overdo anything."

Her "what's your problem" attitude kind of ticked me off. I hadn't asked her to attend this party. In fact, I had conned my best friend into flying over to Europe to accompany me to it, just so Sophie would not have to leave the hospital. Yet here she was, pushing her way back into the investigation, despite our boss's and her doctor's insistence that she stay out of it.

Yet instead of flying off the handle, I tried to put myself in her shoes. Sophie must have been going stir crazy lying in that lonely hospital room, waiting for her bones to heal. Her fretting that Rhonda would sully her reputation couldn't have helped. Still, I had to be the voice of reason.

"Rhonda flew over to help out so you didn't have to exert yourself."

Sophie snorted in a posh sort of way. "Well, that didn't go so well, did it? It's a good thing I arrived when I did, otherwise you would have been removed before you'd had a chance to view the artwork."

She was right, but her snappish attitude didn't help garner more sympathy from me. "Yes, well, I may have overestimated Rhonda's ability to blend in here."

My partner raised a perfectly plucked eyebrow. "May have?"

"Give me a break. Cyril's no Picasso—he paints copies of other artists' works, not originals. I figured he would be interested in a show about collectibles."

My partner clicked her tongue against her palate. "Don't you understand—Cyril sees himself as a true artist, worthy of the same respect as those he copies. Leave him to me. I've dealt with him before and can wind him around my pinky, given the chance."

I nodded, knowing she had a far better chance of success than Rhonda or I. And if the Baroness was keeping Cyril occupied, there was less of a chance that he would notice me snooping around.

"Alright, that sounds like a plan."

I looked towards the gallery door, knowing I needed to get inside so I could examine the works and keep an eye on my bestie. Hopefully the Texans had taken Rhonda under their wing again and would help shield her from our host and his fury, in case of another *faux pas*.

"Look, Sophie, I appreciate your help with Cyril, but please do take it easy tonight."

I gave her hand a quick squeeze before striding ahead to find my friend. However, her next remark stopped me in my tracks.

"Now that I am here, you can tell Rhonda to leave."

I circled back to the Baroness. I should have known she had more than one reason to attend this party. Based on our brief video chats since her hospitalization, it was clear that she was not pleased Rhonda had impressed our boss so quickly. Probably because Sophie had gone on several assignments before Reggie offered her an employment contract. And yet, after Rhonda's first impromptu assignment, she'd proved herself a capable ally; from what Myrtle had said, Reggie was ready to ask my friend to join the team. He just wanted to meet with her first and talk to her about the position in person. Even though Myrtle had told me this in confidence, I had a sneaking suspicion that she had also shared the news with my partner.

"I can't tell Rhonda to leave, just because you showed up. You should be in bed—not rolling around a fancy dress party. She's here to bid on the paintings for Rosewood, and by golly, that is what she is going to do."

I eyed my partner as I spoke, wondering what concerned her more—me being able to complete my job or the potential damage to her reputation.

"But I can bid on them, instead. I don't want to risk Rhonda saying something offensive to Cyril and getting you kicked out, before you can figure out how he is moving stolen art across international boundaries."

So it was both. I held up a hand, stopping her midrant. "I don't know why you decided to disobey your doctor's orders and come to this shindig, but she is staying, so you better be nice to her. Rhonda might not be one of 'your kind,'" I wrapped finger quotations around the last two words, "but she is not uncouth, as you called her."

The Baroness's jaw tightened, but she kept her tone neutral. "I'll apologize for that remark, but not for being here."

"Good, see that you do before the night is over. Rhonda is a good person," I added, hating that I had to keep trying to convince my partner that my best friend did mean well.

The Baroness's chin jutted up. "Just keep her away from Cyril, and we might stand a chance of accomplishing our task tonight. I'm going to mingle with 'my kind,'" she said as she copied my gesture, a smile playing on her lips as she did, "and see if I can find out anything useful. Good luck."

4

A True Artist

My partner hadn't gotten far when a female voice rang out. "Oh, my! Lady Sophie, you poor dear, what has happened to you?"

Sophie gestured for her nurse to turn her around by twisting one hand in the air. I did the same, taking in Countess Ursula, sashaying her way towards us in a blood-red, body-hugging velvet dress and silver boa. She easily balanced on heels so high, I couldn't imagine that she could actually drive her little MGB Roadster with them on.

"Countess Ursula—you were invited?" The Baroness didn't even try to disguise her surprise.

Ursula narrowed her eyes and tossed one end of her boa over her shoulder before answering in a purr of a voice. "Of course. I've bought several lost works from Cyril over the years, pieces that once belonged to my family. He always invites me to his special events."

I hid my grin, knowing that the Baroness had had to practically beg our host for an invitation. Apparently he was quite finicky about who was invited to this annual auction, and most of the guests were long-term clients. Although Cyril and the Baroness were amicable at parties, she had never purchased any of his reproductions, so far as I knew. I couldn't blame her. Why would she want to buy a copy of an old master? Her family hadn't lost anything during the war and she could easily afford to buy the real thing.

When Ursula turned to me, she squinted momentarily as if she was trying to place me. "Oh, yes, I see you brought that journalist with you. I wonder: does Cyril know what your guest does for a living, Sophie?"

My partner ticked her tongue against her teeth. "Carmen works for an antiques magazine, not *The New York Times*. Besides, she's only here to document my purchases for her readers—but only the sales I give her permission to write about," my partner countered, obviously hoping to put the Countess in her place before she shared my background with the host.

I pushed on without saying goodbye, figuring the two minor royals would need a few more minutes to cut each other down before entering the gallery. Technically a countess was smidgen higher than a baroness in the royal rankings, but not by enough for it to matter to Sophie. If Ursula had been a princess, well, then that would have been a different story. I'd met enough major royals while standing by Sophie's side to know how deferential she could be, when necessary.

As I approached the entrance to the gallery, my stomach clenched when I examined the keypad by the door. It was a new and expensive model, and one I would not easily circumvent, at least not without drawing attention to myself. Yet if I was going to have any chance of examining the artwork alone, I needed to figure out the combination.

However, since I doubted our host would up and tell me the code, I would have to think up a wilier method of getting back inside. I could always drop my favorite lipstick, so that Cyril would have to let me in again, later. Yet considering his grumpy attitude towards me, I would rather think up another way in, one that didn't draw attention to myself or require his cooperation or knowledge.

So I pushed my frustration with the keypad aside and mentally prepared for the main event. When I entered the auction space, my jaw dropped slightly as my eyes took in the sight before me.

Cyril Bouve may have been a pompous jerk, but he was one heck of a painter.

Hanging across from the entrance was a man dressed in monk's clothes, smiling at me as he hoisted a beer. His jovial expression, as well as the rapid brushstrokes used to paint the man's clothing and face, told me that I was staring at a replica of a Frans Hals painting.

A brightly colored oil, as tall as I was, hung next to the portrait. The abstract depiction of three women—naked save for the masks covering their faces—could only be a missing work by Pablo Picasso. Farther down the wall, a small sketch in a large frame drew me to it. Heavy, dark lines formed a woman's body, stretched out on a chaise lounge as she smiled up at the artist, who was clearly Henri Matisse.

I leaned in so close my nose practically touched the piece. The artist had made several "reclining nude" sketches, making them easily recognizable. Cyril's reproduction seemed perfect. Yet, the longer I looked at it, the more I realized that a few of the lines were a bit wobbly. Only slightly, but enough to be noticeable. Was the original also so? It could have been; Matisse made so many of them they couldn't have all been perfect. Yet I did not recall Matisse's lines ever being so uneven. I pulled back to study it from a different angle. Was Cyril losing his touch, or had he simply rushed the job? Johnny did mention that Cyril had been late with finishing these copies. I would have to search for photos of the original to compare them to this one.

I quickly counted twenty canvases, painted in a vast range of styles and genres. Cyril really could turn his hand to anything, I thought, admiring his work. It would be a shame if he ended up rotting in jail again, instead of being able to keep creating such wonderful paintings. Nevertheless, I was not here to sentence the man, but only to search for evidence. It could be that Cyril was not involved with a smuggling ring, after all.

Next to each work was a short description, the painting's title, its maker, and the year the original disappeared. Each had been framed in the style appropriate to the era in which it had been painted. He had even added the appropriate amount of craquelure and yellowing varnish to the older works, making them appear to have aged with time.

For a brief moment, I forgot about my assignment and simply enjoyed standing here, while taking in these precious paintings. However, I couldn't really get lost in his work until I had finished mine. So I set off to complete my task. After double-checking that the hidden camera mounted inside of my dragonfly pin's eyes was aimed correctly, I circled the space, snapping photos of the guests and paintings as I went. Luckily it was an attractive piece of jewelry, and several guests stopped to look closely at it, giving me excellent closeups of their faces. I was nervous the pinhole camera would be detected, but so far, no one seemed to notice. It did help that the jeweler had modified both eyes, so that they matched.

As soon as I had documented everyone and everything, I turned towards one wall, so as to have a little more privacy, and then sent the photos off to Myrtle. I didn't really need to worry about anyone spying on me, I realized after noting that several guests had phones to their ears or in their hands. Most were probably contacting their art consultants and trying to work out whether any of the paintings were a sound investment.

The exclusiveness and secrecy surrounding this annual auction most likely accounted for its popularity among Cyril's clients. He never publicized the sale, always kept the titles and artists of the to-be-sold works a secret, and guaranteed that these paintings were one-offs—meaning he would never copy them again or sell lithographs of them.

And therein lay the problem. Our source claimed to have seen multiple copies of the same painting during a previous auction held in Venice, yet both disappeared from the gallery before our agents could confirm the intel. And recently, two of the originals that Cyril had made copies of for previous Lost Masterpieces auctions had been found during Mafia-related police raids in Italy and Croatia. Yet neither of those works had been stolen during World War II; rather, they'd gone missing during art heists committed the year before he had auctioned off his repeats of those paintings.

Was it a coincidence that the recovered works had been copied by Cyril and sold through his annual auction a few months before the genuine works resurfaced? It could be, but I didn't believe in them. And neither did my boss, which was why I was here.

Before I could hit "send" on the last batch of photos, out of the corner of my eye, I saw Ursula and Cyril approaching fast on my left, their arms interlocked and their heads close together. So I kept my gaze fixed on the wonderfully serene landscape by Paul Cezanne before me. Luckily for me, Ursula was also intrigued by the canvas.

"Oh, Cyril, you have outdone yourself this time," Countess Ursula cooed. "I am in love with that Cezanne. It's simply breathtaking."

He straightened up, and blushes of pink soon colored his cheeks. "Yes, well, I am also quite pleased with how this year's selection turned out."

I agreed completely, but felt as if I couldn't tell him that. The man made me nervous, and I was afraid I would say something I would regret. Right now, I wanted to do everything to avoid attracting his attention. So I casually moved away from the pair so I could complete my task.

Only after I had sent all of the photos of the guests and paintings to Myrtle, marking my first chore complete, did I allow myself to get lost in Cyril's work. I devoured each canvas, greedily taking in the plethora of styles, each so well executed I had trouble believing the same two hands had created everything in this room. I could also see how his work had fooled so many experts for so many years. It felt as if I was staring at better works by big-name artists such as Cezanne, Monet, Picasso, and Matisse. And each was as well done as the next.

Cyril certainly lived up to his reputation as an incredibly talented forger. In a way, I better understood his refusal to be painted off as nothing but a copy artist.

For a brief moment, I felt a wave of sadness roll over me as I regarded his work. Part of me hoped that our intel was wrong and that Cyril was simply the victim of an overactive imagination or sick vendetta. That wouldn't be the first time someone had tipped the Rosewood Agency off about a stolen work, only for us to discover that the person in question was as honest as they came. It would be interesting to see how this investigation panned out, and whether Cyril was as dirty as my boss hoped.

5

Question Time

I pulled my eyes away from the canvases, reminding myself that I was here to study the invitees as well as the paintings. Yet before I could decide who to corner first, Cyril's voice rang out, determining my path. He had been mingling ever since the gallery door opened and was clearly pleased to see that everyone was enthusiastic about his latest works.

"Are you satisfied with your latest delivery?" I overheard him asking the trio of Spanish investors, who had been having an animated discussion while standing in front of a work originally by Paul Gauguin.

"Yes, the selection of Warhol prints you chose fit in perfectly with our last hotel's interior design. We hope you can help us again with another project. We're opening a new resort in Bali next year and are considering using your reproductions to decorate it."

Cyril's hand flew to his heart as he bowed deeply before the three Spaniards. "It would be an honor to work with you again. Have your project manager reach out to my assistant whenever you have a concept for the interiors and I'll get to work."

My research had made clear that despite his website's proclamation that his primary source of income was his commissioned work, in reality it was the far cheaper prints he offered in bulk. The prints were high-quality reproductions of his forged paintings, which I assume he did to ensure that no copyright laws had been broken. From what I'd seen online, they were printed on thick paper and framed well enough to be hung in high-end office buildings, hotels, casinos, hospitals, and the like.

The eldest Spaniard gestured at the copy of the Gauguin behind them, a tropical scene painted during the artist's Tahitian period. Cyril Bouve's name was boldly painted where Gauguin's should have been.

"This piece would be perfect. Is it possible to order two hundred reproductions of it tonight?"

Cyril sighed deeply. "I am sorry, but I meant what I said earlier. The works in this room are unique. I refuse to make another copy or sell reproductions of them—they are too special. That is also why I am asking more for these pieces than I do for a commissioned piece."

"I see; it is a disappointment, but understandable."

It was a disappointment to me, too. If they were truly unique, why did Reggie's informant see multiple copies of the same piece at last year's Lost Masterpieces auction? I couldn't ask the host, so I remained quiet and kept listening in.

Cyril patted him on the back, as if they were old friends. "I'm certain we can find something else that suits your style and tastes. You should come by the gallery on Monday and I can show you several examples that I believe will meet with your satisfaction."

"Excellent." After the eldest man agreed to Cyril's plan, he returned his attention to his two companions, and they began speaking in Spanish again.

The artist stepped away from the trio and announced, "I am glad to see that you are all enjoying the show. In a few minutes, we will return to the lounge for the first round of bidding. If anyone has any questions about my pieces or the missing originals, please do let me know."

I practically ran over to the portly man, wanting to ask a few questions before he was inundated with them.

"Do you really sign the back of each painting?" I breathed as soon as I was within hearing range.

"Of course I do! Otherwise someone might get the wrong idea and think I was trying to pass them off as the real artist's work. Which I no longer do," he said loudly, punctuating his attempt at a joke with a hearty chortle.

To prove his point, he strode over to the nearest painting and pulled it off the single wire holding it to the wall. I was happy to see that there were no extra security precautions taken—because, I assumed, we were inside a heavily guarded free port. I got as close as I could to the painting, without getting in Cyril's personal space, eager to see whether I would notice anything off about the canvas or frame.

Yet to my disappointment, the frame was definitely not thick enough to hold a rolled-up original, and the canvas visible on the back was clearly new material that had been recently mounted onto the stretcher frame—the formal name for the wooden frame that the canvas was stretched over and stapled or nailed onto, to ensure that the front of the painting remained flat and taut.

I wondered whether the creases on the corners and folded sides had hardened into place, which only happened after many years of being nailed in the same position. I dared not touch it and test my theory in front of our host, but I did make a mental note to do so later. Yet from this quick visual examination, I believed that this painting was not an old masterpiece with Cyril's flamboyant signature added to the back, but a new canvas that had recently been stretched onto this frame.

He held up the painting so that everyone could see the back, which was entirely covered with his signature, despite the shortness of his name. "See, that proves that it's mine."

Well, I guess I can cross that theory off my list, I thought. Luckily for my boss, I still had a few more ideas to test. But to do so, I'd need some alone time with these works.

"Your paintings are beautiful and so diverse, qua style and execution. Do you work from the originals?" I knew it was a stupid question, but that was the point. Sometimes playing dumb had its advantages. The more people underestimated me, the more I could get away with, right under their noses, without them ever suspecting me. He already thought so little of me; I didn't want to give him a reason to think I was smart enough to catch on to anything illicit he may be up to.

Cyril threw up his hands before answering me in a tone fit for a precocious two-year-old. "Of course not! They are missing works, as in no one knows where they are. Are you certain that you and Lady Sophie were acquainted before her accident? She is obviously taking quite a few painkillers at the moment. That might explain why she insisted that you and that TV person take her place."

I decided to ignore his blatant insult and instead asked another obtuse question.

"If these paintings are missing, how do you know what they look like?"

He pinched the bridge of his nose and shook his head. I swear he was about to walk away without answering, at least until his cruise ship-owning friends moseyed over.

"We were wondering the same thing," Gary said. He and his wife took large sips of their freshly topped-off pints and looked to the artist, clearly waiting for him to answer.

Our host took a moment to compose himself before answering, apparently aware that he couldn't treat his longtime clients as buffoons, if he wanted to keep their business.

"I rely on old photographs that I find in books and online to re-create them."

"How do you decide which paintings to copy?" Gary asked.

Cyril cringed.

"I mean, to make a repeat of."

"I take inspiration from the many art loss databases available online. When I find one that speaks to me, I paint it. It's that simple."

"Well, these certainly spoke to you because they are gorgeous. I would almost think Gauguin, Cezanne, and Matisse had really created those," I blurted out.

The corner of his lips turned downward. "Almost?"

"The old masters have something about them, a luminosity if you will, because of the way the paint ages over the centuries that, I suppose, simply cannot be replicated. Yours breathes new life into them—that is for certain—but it is new life, isn't it?"

I tried to keep my tone philosophical, but it wasn't going to work. I was starting to think that if Rhonda didn't get us kicked out, I would. There was just something about this man that made me tongue-tied and nervous. I didn't know whether it was his jittery way of continually adjusting his scarf, or his constant glasses cleaning, or his habit of continually clearing his throat in a way that made you think he was about to give a speech. He just put me on edge.

Cyril's face paled rapidly, and I feared he was going to eject me from the party right then and there. Luckily, the Westworths asked another question before he could.

"Why are you holding this auction inside of the free port, instead of your gallery?" Trish asked.

"It's easier for the winners to move their artwork around Europe without having to pay extra transport fees or taxes."

"Why is that?" I batted my eyelashes and feigned incompetence, hoping he would explain what he was doing in such a way that I might see where the loophole was.

By the way Cyril sucked in his breath and narrowed his eyes, I suspected his patience with me had run out. Luckily he was too polite—at least in front of Gary and Trish—to ignore my question.

"The taxes on their purchases are paid only after they leave the free zone, at their final destinations when customs clears them. Because the climate-controlled facilities are suitable for fine art, the new owners can store them here for as long as they want to. That gives them time to decide in which of their many homes they want to display their paintings, without incurring extra transportation fees, or having to worry about its condition or the insurance, until they do," Cyril explained.

"That makes sense," I said, but the English couple were suspiciously quiet.

When Cyril looked over, he too seemed to notice that Gary and Trish were no longer listening, but looking around as if they were searching for another quarrel to entertain them. That meant question time was over, as far as I was concerned. Technically, I had not been invited to the party, but was here as Rhonda's plus one, so I couldn't really complain.

He bowed slightly to the cruise-ship couple, excluding me from his gaze and gesture. "Now, if you will excuse me, I wish you luck with the bidding."

6

An Indecent Proposal

Cyril didn't wait for the Westworths to reply, but immediately set off in the opposite direction. At least, he attempted to. A few steps in, he seemed to swoon for a moment, as if he was about to lose his balance. Cyril was pushing seventy, I remembered; we all get a little wobbly with age.

When he leaned one hand against the wall for support, Manzino crossed over to him, a concerned expression on his face. However, once he reached our host, he pulled Cyril roughly towards one corner of the room. Based on the men's animated and irritated gestures, it was obviously not a social chat.

I homed in on the two, mentally mapping the easiest way to reach them, while keeping my back to them, just as Rhonda grabbed ahold of my arm.

"Isn't this wonderful! Cyril is quite talented," my bestie gushed.

"Yes, he really is," I said in a booming voice, before adding in a whisper, "Excuse me, I want to listen in on a conversation. I'll be right back."

Rhonda's eyes widened. "You're on the job now, aren't you? How exciting! Good luck."

I winced at her enthusiasm and the volume of her voice. *The Baroness may be right; I'll have to ask Rhonda to be a bit more discreet about my reasons for being here.*

The two men were standing next to a vibrant work originally by Marc Chagall, giving me a reason to get close. Hopefully I could pretend to be so lost in the beauty of the painting that neither man would notice me.

"Oh, there's that Chagall you'd mentioned. I'm going to take a closer look. Be right back," I said a shade too loudly.

"Great idea. I'm going to ask Josie and Johnny what they think of that landscape by Caspar David Friedrich. I do love the German romantic period," Rhonda replied and winked at me conspiratorially.

Yep, I was going to have to ask her to tone it down before the Baroness noticed her behavior and ticked me on the fingers for it. Or, worse, told Reggie about it.

I sashayed my way over to the Chagall, as quickly as I could without drawing attention to myself. Whatever the two men were discussing was irritating our host to the point where I wondered how much longer Cyril would stand there before he either exploded or walked away.

Just as I was positioning myself in front of the Chagall, with my back to the two men but close enough to overhear their words, Cyril cried out, "Enough! I've told you before, this is not the right time or place to discuss this—I'm right in the middle of hosting a party and auction! We can talk later. Now, if you will excuse me…"

Drat! Too late, I scolded myself, regretting that I had let Rhonda keep me from moving in closer sooner. I kept my eyes on the painting but could see Cyril walking into my peripheral vision as he passed me by, when his Italian counterpart grabbed his arm again.

"Your guests are busy looking at the artwork. You have time now. Anyway, it's your fault I'm here. We should be having this auction in my gallery, not in this free port. But you refused to deliver the paintings, as agreed—and then you try and ignore me? If you'd answered my emails or returned my calls, I wouldn't have to confront you like this."

"It took more time to complete all of the pictures, that's all," Cyril said sulkily. "I have a plan in place to ensure that your work gets to Italy, don't worry."

Nico began to protest, but stopped midsentence and grew so quiet, I thought he was about to walk away from Cyril. However, I heard no footsteps, so I resisted the urge to turn around and see what the two men were doing, in the hopes that Nico would soon continue. A few seconds later, I was rewarded for my patience. Yet when he spoke again, his tone had softened considerably. "What do you think of my proposal?"

Cyril shook his head vehemently. "I read through your ridiculous proposition, but I cannot agree to any of the insulting terms discussed within it."

"Why not? I'm giving you a great deal. You want to retire, and this would be your pension plan. All you have to do is keep signing your name to them."

"You cannot be serious! The works your crew creates are far from perfect."

"They don't need to be perfect!"

"Yes, they do, if they bear my name. I am an artist, after all," Cyril countered. I could almost see him jutting out his chin as he said it.

"No, you are a convicted forger who sells reproductions to make ends meet. You don't make originals, remember? So why are you being so bullheaded about this? If we do it my way, we both win."

"I want my son, Cyprus, to take over my gallery, not your gang of mediocre copy artists." In my peripheral vision, I could see Cyril's head turning towards a squat man who could have been his father's twin, instead of his offspring. Cyprus's decision to dress in a tuxedo fit for a 1920s butler didn't help him look any younger. Rhonda and I had spoken to him briefly earlier, and I had to agree with my friend that he was as interesting a conversation partner as a stack of pancakes probably would be.

"Cyprus is not interested in painting reproductions, as I do. He wants to branch out and make original artwork in the style of famous artists. He is far more creative than I ever was, yet has my ability to replicate any artist he chooses. It's a thing of beauty to see him paint."

"That will ruin everything! We have created the perfect method to accomplish our goals—why must you mess with it? Can you talk with him about—"

"I refuse to manipulate him, especially for your boss! Cyprus should have the freedom to do what he wants and not be restrained, as I was. I had no choice but to copy other artists because that is what my artistic gift is—but he does. Besides, I've made enough money since I was released from prison that my son will never want for anything."

"Now, if you will excuse me…" Cyril repeated.

"I can arrange for you to receive a bigger cut, and I'll send up my best artists to work under your tutelage…"

"No, it's too late for all of that. My mind is made up."

Manzino was quiet a moment, before stating in an even lower tone, "The men I work for don't like to hear the word no."

Alarm bells went off in my head. When a suspected criminal of Italian heritage uttered those words, my first thought was—the Mafia. Yet I had no time to contemplate Manzino's deeper meaning, for Cyril had apparently had enough.

"How dare you come to my party and threaten me! Leave me alone. I have guests to attend to."

"There you are," Margreta, Cyril's party planner, called out as she rushed over to her boss. She held up her phone's screen. "It is time to return to the lounge for the first round of bidding."

"Excellent, I cannot wait to see what my paintings bring in. Margreta, let's round up the guests. Manzino, if you will excuse us."

Cyril adjusted his glasses before nodding to his Italian counterpart, who was acting quite cordial, now that they had company.

"Certainly." The Italian held up his glass, as if to toast our host. "Good luck."

I watched as Cyril and Margreta jovially tapped several guests on the shoulders and asked them to return to the other room. The artist seemed to have already shaken off his fight with Manzino.

As I replayed their conversation in my mind, I thought of how ironic it would have been for an artist famous for making copies of important art to sign his name on work he had not painted.

Try as I might to twist their words, nothing they had said indicated that they were smuggling paintings. And I still didn't understand why the Mafia would be so interested in Cyril's repeats. A genuine masterpiece could be used to broker a deal or pay off a debt, but not a copy of one. Instead of providing answers, all their conversation did was raise new questions.

Maybe Cyril's secret wasn't that he was smuggling originals, but that he was selling more than one copy of his purportedly unique line of paintings. That would explain why Reggie's informant had seen two copies of the same work.

I definitely had new intel to share with Rosewood, but couldn't draw any conclusions from it yet. Still, it was worth sending an update to Myrtle so that she could mull this information over, as well. She was one of the smartest people I knew and might see a connection that I did not.

7

Myrtle Sends an Update

I considered sharing my findings with the Baroness, but now was not the time to do so. The space was far too public for me to approach her stealthily, and I'd just learned how easy it was to be overheard. The last thing I wanted to do was make our host suspect that she was up to something sinister, or that I was anything more than an assistant to her.

Before I could decide what to do next, my phone pinged, its sound slightly muffled by my Fendi purse. I dug it out, hoping to see my company contact's name on the screen. Sure enough, it was a message from Myrtle and quite a long one at that, at least for her doing.

Her team was still working on background checks on all of the guests, but they had already identified all twenty paintings. Fifteen were indeed lost during World War Two, as our illustrious host had stated. But five had not gone missing during the war, but had been lifted from private museums in more recent robberies that the police suspected had been executed by several different European criminal organizations.

I knew from their titles and short descriptions exactly which pieces she meant. The five odd ones out were a small landscape by Paul Cezanne, the sketch by Matisse that I had been admiring, an adorable portrait of a young girl playing in a garden by Edouard Manet, a rugged landscape by Caspar David Friedrich, and a view of a Venetian canal painted by Canaletto in the 1700s that was so serene, it calmed my soul just by looking at it.

I was initially shocked that Myrtle had discovered this information so quickly, until I recalled that all she had to do was search our art loss database for the title. Cyril claimed to do extensive research into the pieces he painted, before he even picked up a brush. So why did he lie about those five paintings' backstories? This was definitely a mystery I needed to solve.

When Margreta approached me with a thin smile on her lips, I knew what she was going to ask. "Madame, would you join us in the lounge? It's time for the first round of bidding."

"Of course." I shielded my phone from her view, stifling a sigh as I did. How I longed for the days when strangers called me "miss" instead of "madame."

As I trailed after the others, I let my mind work through the puzzle before me. Ever since Cyril had shown us the back of one of his paintings, I had been mulling over how he could have disguised the original pieces or altered them in some way, so that they appeared to be made by him.

From what I could see with the naked eye, the paint across the entire canvas seemed too new for him to have simply painted over the signature. But if he had painted over the whole thing, he was taking an enormous risk. It was a complicated and challenging process to remove so much overpainting without damaging the original layers underneath. The chance was far greater that he'd ruin it in the process, rendering it worthless.

Yet, the genuine versions of two paintings he had replicated had been recently found in the hands of high-ranking Mafia members. If he wasn't painting over the originals, how else could he have gotten them down to Italy?

I tapped my chin, considering another possibility. Were the recovered paintings really the originals? Or was an overeager art specialist trying to help the cops pin a higher sentence on the criminal by declaring one of Cyril's fakes to be genuine?

Part of me wanted to fly down to Italy and examine the confiscated work myself, but I knew Reggie wouldn't allow it, not if it implied that I mistrusted the law enforcement officers.

So I messaged Myrtle, instead. "Are we certain the confiscated artwork is genuine? Could you look into it for me, please?" I added a blushing face emoji on the end. There was no time to explain my theory in full. For that I would have to wait until we were back in the hotel.

Just as I was starting to lose hope that Cyril was smuggling anything, a single word drifted into my ear, causing me to salivate. Why did the word "stolen" illicit such a Pavlovian reaction in me?

8

Hold Your Horses

I had just entered the lounge when Johnny's voice rose up above the jazzy music playing softly through the speakers, and the din of chatting guests.

"Of course we didn't know it was recently stolen! I told you before, and I'll tell you again—I'm no thief. Now get away from us!"

Gary and Trish were standing close to the doorway, partially blocking my view of the rest. When I stood on my tippy toes so I could peer over Gary's shoulder, I could see the Texan getting into a disagreement with someone I didn't recognize. I would have said that it was another invited guest, except for the fact that this person was no more than thirty years old and was dressed in a dirty pair of jeans and a dusty T-shirt.

Their argument seemed to be escalating, as were their gestures and tones, until I saw Johnny push the younger man away. "I don't know anything about that. How dare you accuse me or my wife of breaking the law!"

He looked around the room until he spotted our host.

"Hey Cyril, who let this guy in? This is the same person I told you about—the one who's been spreading nasty rumors about me. And now he's threatening to blackmail me, too!"

Johnny glared at the person in question, who met his gaze defiantly. The young man gestured around the room, as if he was addressing all of the guests. "I know what all of you are doing here!"

"I don't know where you get your intel from, buddy, but I don't buy stolen art. And I don't want you to go spreading lies around that I do," the Texan growled.

Cyril pushed his way through the crowd, freezing when he saw who the Texans were arguing with. "Enrico, what are you doing here? I fired you last week. You have no right to be here."

"I told you I would get you back. You had no right to treat me so badly."

The young man looked as if he was about to burst into tears, but his emotional state didn't seem to affect Cyril. The artist simply glared at him as he called out, "Margreta!"

When his assistant appeared by his elbow seconds later, Cyril said in a calm voice, "Please contact security. I want this man escorted out of the building immediately."

"No! I refuse to leave until you compensate me. I deserve more money if you want me to keep quiet."

"Compensate you?" He turned to the young man, hands on his hips. "You stole from me, remember? You shouldn't have come here. You're a deranged thief, and apparently also an extortionist. Why would you accuse my loyal clients of purchasing stolen art? I make copies—nothing in that gallery is an original."

I had to suppress a snort at our prideful host's sudden modesty.

But Cyril was oblivious to any shame in his admission and kept his head held high. "If you leave quietly, I will not press charges."

Enrico raised his fist into the air as if he wanted to make another proclamation, but something in his facial expression told me he was waffling. Ultimately he let his hand fall and leaned in to Cyril. "If you want me to hold my tongue, you will have to pay me more—one way or the other. Otherwise I'm telling the police everything. I'll be seeing you, old man."

He tugged on Cyril's scarf, sending it wafting to the ground, then strode towards the door. We all watched as the young man exited as quickly as he had entered, his head held high the entire time. Our host scooped up his silky shawl before rushing after him, screaming for security as he did. Considering the security measures taken inside this building, I was certain Enrico would be restrained and ejected as soon as someone heard Cyril bellowing.

"What was that all about?" I asked the Texans.

"That young buck seems to think some of the works sold at these auctions are not painted by Cyril, but are stolen works he's passing off as his own. And he's gotten it into his head that I bought a few them last year, knowing they were stolen." Johnny pushed up his hat to scratch at his forehead. "I think it's all bull-honkey and that the kid's got no proof."

"Who is he?" I asked.

Johnny shook his head. "I do not know, but I'm going to find out."

Before he could make a move, Cyril strode back inside and closed the door firmly behind him.

"Who was that awful man?" Countess Ursula asked.

Was Enrico telling the truth? was, to me, the more pressing question, but I doubted anyone at this party would dare to vocalize it in front of our host.

"Enrico's worked in my framing department for several years. I had high hopes for his future, but I recently discovered that he has been stealing expensive supplies and reselling them for a profit. I fired him last week, and he's been trouble ever since."

Cyril's arrogant tone dissolved slightly as he spoke, and I actually sensed remorse in his voice, albeit briefly. But was what he'd said about Enrico true?

Enrico seemed to be implying that Cyril was somehow involved in the smuggling of stolen art and assumed that his clients knew it, as well. He must have seen something he was not supposed to while at work, something that made him believe Cyril was engaged in illicit activities. I would have to try to contact the young man later. Hopefully he would be able—and willing—to shed more light on how Cyril was moving the stolen paintings around Europe.

"How in tarnation did that young man get inside of this fortress?" Josie asked.

Cyril shook his head. "He must have shown them his employee badge. I had it deactivated, but didn't think to take it back from him. I suppose I should have. But I assure you all that he will no longer be a problem. The security here is top-notch."

Our host was less upset, and more contemplative, about the appearance of his thieving employee than I would have expected, given the accusations that had been made. Yet soon the vague wash over his eyes seemed to dissolve, and he snapped back to attention. "My dear guests, let's try to ignore this strange turn of events and get back to the reason for our being here—the silent auction!"

9

Round One

A round of clapping confirmed that the guests were ready to move on, as well.

Cyril brightened visibly. "Excellent. Let's begin the first round of bidding. You will notice the boxes placed on tables spread around the room. Each has a—"

"Cyril, you don't need to explain how to everyone. I still don't see Serena, which means I'm planning on outbidding you all." Johnny's boast got a polite chuckle from his small crowd.

"You're as bad as Serena is, Bighorn," Gary balked. "Give us a chance to win a bid, without us having to sell a cruise ship to pay for it."

"Gary is right, Johnny. In the spirit of fair play, you should give others a chance to win. But really, everyone here can afford to bid far over the reserve price, can't they?" Cyril said with a wink, getting a genuine laugh out of his guests.

Myrtle was slowly putting names to faces, and the information about the invitees was trickling in. So far, pretty much everyone present was Fortune 500 material. Seeing as the combined net worth of the invitees at this party was in the high billions if not trillions, I was certain Cyril was correct in his assessment. Yet, as I had often noted, the absurdly wealthy usually didn't want to give out a penny more than they needed to, unless it was absolutely necessary.

"And I should let you know that Serena is on her way, and I expect her to arrive any minute. So do keep that in mind when placing your bid. I will also ask her to limit the number of paintings she bids on, but I can't guarantee that she'll show restraint when deciding on how much to bid."

"In other words, don't go too low—am I right?" Josie said with a laugh.

"How does this silent auction work?" one of the Spanish gentlemen asked.

"As I was saying, there are boxes placed around the room for you to deposit your bid slip into." Cyril gestured towards the small wooden boxes resting on several tables, each with a laminated reproduction of the artwork to be bid on glued to the front of it.

"Do not forget to put your unique bidder's code and bid amount on each slip of paper. I would also like to know which free port you would prefer to take the painting out at, so I can arrange for the transportation tonight. There will be two rounds of bidding. The highest bids from the first round will be revealed before we have another viewing and a second round of bidding. As our finale, I'll announce the winners over a glass of France's finest champagne!"

My heart leapt when he mentioned a second viewing. That gave me a second chance to try to photograph the key code. All I had to do was ensure I was standing next to him when he punched it in.

Cyril picked up a slip of paper from one of several stacks placed on the tables. "You can use a different slip of paper for each bid. Feel free to look up prices online or phone a friend—I don't care, as long as you don't post about this auction on social media until it's over. Otherwise, this will be your last invitation to one of my parties."

I breathed a sigh of relief, thankful that Cyril didn't have an aversion to us using our phones, and even encouraged the buyers to call their consultants. It would make it easier to get in touch with Myrtle and share intel, without drawing attention to myself.

"You must be serious if you're threatened to banish us from your future soirees," Trish joked.

"I am." Neither Cyril's tone or expression held a hint of a smile. "I'll make the highest bids known in a half-hour. There are nibbles and bubbles circulating to keep you refreshed and sated until then. Good luck."

After he clicked his heels and bowed to his audience, Rhonda leaned over and whispered, "That's funny—I thought there was only one round of bidding during a silent auction."

I kept my eyes pointed forward as I answered her in a soft voice. "Usually you would be right. In this case, I believe he's trying to drive the prices up even higher by adding in a second round. If one of the guests is waffling on bidding on a certain piece, but then sees that it's quite desired, they may be tempted to bid on it during the second round, even if they aren't really in love with it. Meanwhile, another guest may bid more than they'd initially planned to during the second round, perhaps even against themselves, simply to ensure that they win."

Rhonda nodded once, then added too loudly. "That makes sense. Say, can I do anything to help with your mission?"

I sucked in a breath, hoping the Baroness and our host were too far away to have heard her remark. If Cyril got the idea that I was here on an assignment or mission—of any sort—I was certain he would eject me as quickly as he had the framer.

I took a look around to ensure that our host was not within earshot, but couldn't find him. Granted, he was a head shorter than most of the guests, especially those in astronomically high heels. Sure enough, on a second sweep, I spotted him chatting with Countess Ursula, towering over him in her feathery ensemble. I'd almost missed him because she had her head bent down so Cyril could whisper something in her ear. Whatever it was, her mischievous smile grew tenfold the longer he spoke.

"Certainly," was her rather loud response to a question I could not hear.

Moments later, Manzino interrupted their conversation and pulled our host aside. I was far too far away to hear it all, but the Italian was clearly upset as he gestured repeatedly towards the door. Did this have something to do with the framer and the accusations he'd leveled at both our host and the invitees?

Since I couldn't get any closer without drawing attention to myself, I decided to brief Rhonda on my plan, instead. "I'm going to do a little mingling in a minute, but first, let's talk about the bids. I would like you to place bids on these five paintings, but let the rest be."

I handed her my phone, its screen filled with the titles and artists of the pieces Myrtle had singled out.

However, she didn't even look at the screen. Instead, she glanced at the Baroness before her eyes dropped to the floor. "Are you certain you want me to bid on the paintings? Now that Lady Sophie is here, I thought she would—"

"No!" I said, a little too harshly. "This is your assignment. You flew all the way over here to help me out. She should be in the hospital and knows it, but is too stubborn to admit it. We stick to our plan, alright?"

Before we arrived at the auction, I had already asked Rhonda to be prepared to bid on a few items tonight, and had even arranged access to Rosewood's reserve funds, in case she won. As far as Rhonda knew, my magazine had deep pockets and was willing to go all out because they expected an uptick in subscribers and a new source of ad revenue, as a result of this investigative piece. All lies, of course, but believable in this commercialized age.

Rhonda brightened up again before leaning in too close and whispering conspiratorially. "Alright. Why those five?"

She needed to learn to not act so conspicuous and simply accept her orders if she was to have a future at Rosewood. The way she was behaving attracted more attention than if she had just casually asked me.

"Can you just trust me for now? I'll explain everything when we are somewhere less public. Those are the only five I would like you to bid on." I couldn't tell her the truth, even when we were alone, I feared. There was too great a chance that she'd blab anything I shared with her to another.

She took my phone and read over the titles before handing it back. "Alright. How much should I bid and which free port should I list?"

"Can you please bid ten thousand euros over the reserve prices for each of the five? That will at least get you in the game. We can always up the amount during the second round, if need be."

The five I was interested in were priced between fifty and one hundred thousand dollars, making them among the most expensive of the paintings

Cyril had on offer tonight. With a lot of luck, we might win one bid and thereby get a good look at one of the paintings on Myrtle's list. But it was probably going to take a lot more than a few thousand over the reserve price to come out on top.

Despite my reservations about Rhonda's chances, I grabbed a bidding slip and noted the blank spaces for her bidding number, the bid amount, and preferred port to pick it up from. I thought back to the intel we'd received so far. The stolen art had been found in Italy and Croatia. The free ports of Trieste and Venice were the closest ones, as far as I knew.

"Please put down Italy as the pickup location."

I pulled back and plastered on a smile, just in time to see Cyril crossing over to us, a scowl on his face. *Great, what's got him so upset this time?* I wondered as I pocketed my phone.

"Are you even going to bid on my work, or is it beneath you?" Cyril asked, sarcasm dripping from his voice.

"Why would I be here, otherwise? I need something to decorate my bathroom," Rhonda replied in an equally snotty tone, obviously fed up with our host's rude behavior, derogatory remarks, and superior attitude.

As Rhonda probably expected, Cyril took her comment as an insult. His head wobbled in anger like a dashboard bobblehead. "Why, I never!"

I muttered under my breath, certain he was going to kick us out before Rhonda could place a single bid. Luckily, the Baroness must have heard his gasp, because she had her nurse roll her straight over.

"What happened now?" she said, her question directed more at me than Cyril. However, our host was oblivious to the true nature of our relationship, and assumed she meant him.

"Lady Sophie, you know I adore you, but your guest has been pushing my limits all evening. I do not understand how you can associate yourself with this person."

Her social position required her to smooth over this situation, but I hated that we'd put her in this position again. The way Sophie eyed Rhonda, with a mixture of irritation and revulsion, I truly did wonder what she was going to say. To my relief, whatever nasty thoughts may have been running through her mind, she kept to herself.

"It's a long and rather boring story, but the short of it is, Rhonda recently helped me through a difficult period and I thought she would enjoy taking my place at this auction, so I extended her my invitation as a way of thanking her. Obviously I was wrong." My partner briefly locked eyes with Rhonda before returning her gaze to Cyril.

"I'm not sure what is going through her head this evening, but she is usually not as obtuse as she appears to be acting tonight. It must be the jet lag. I do apologize for her unbecoming behavior."

Out of the corner of my eye, I could see Rhonda's cheeks growing redder by the second.

Sophie may have been looking at Cyril when she spoke, but her words were directed at me. It was the Baroness's equivalent of "I told you so." She had been convinced that my bestie would mess up this assignment, and by golly, she sure seemed to be right.

I sighed in frustration. I had really wanted Rhonda to knock this one out of the park. My boss's enthusiasm for her help during our last, spontaneous recovery mission had me convinced that we might just get to officially work together quite soon. But if things went sideways with this gig, then Reggie wouldn't have any use for her.

Yet Rhonda knew nothing of Reggie's interest in her working for Rosewood, or how upset Sophie really was by her presence here tonight. So she made a point of grabbing a bidding sheet, scribbling her bid onto it, before dropping it into the nearest box.

When Cyril lunged forward, as if he wanted to rip Rhonda's bid out of the box and tear it up, Sophie stopped him in his tracks.

"Cyril, darling, what would you recommend I bid on your Cezanne? I just love how you have captured the light so brilliantly."

For some reason, Cyril didn't seem to want to offend Sophie in any way, which made her far better suited for this assignment than my bestie. Cyril glared at Rhonda and muttered "uncouth" as he followed the Baroness to the other side of the room, but otherwise let us be.

I grabbed Rhonda's elbow and propelled her away from Cyril and towards the bar. "Why don't we get a drink to celebrate your first bid," I said in a bright voice.

I ordered us both a glass of merlot, before leaning over to Rhonda's ear. "I need to do a little work. Can you please bid on the other four and stay out of Cyril's way?" It was going to be challenging to figure out who the players were, if I had to babysit Rhonda the entire evening. And from what I'd just seen, I doubted the Baroness would enjoy keeping her occupied.

Yet by the way Rhonda hung her head, I knew I'd gone too far. After the Baroness's dressing down, she needed a friend, not someone giving her orders. So I bumped her hip with mine. "For a guy who makes reproductions for a living, I had not expected Cyril to be such a snob."

That got a slight chuckle out of my friend. "He really does see himself as a true artist. It is a little odd and definitely unrealistic. He makes copies, for goodness' sake!"

"I agree completely. That's probably why he's doing something illicit on the side, because he couldn't make ends meet, otherwise."

Rhonda hid a smile behind her hand, but I could see her posture straightening out as her confidence returned. I knew she was going to be fine when she gave me a quick hug.

"Thanks, Carmen, you always know what to say. You go do whatever it is you need to do. You can count on me not to upset Cyril."

The determination in her voice told me that I really didn't need to worry about her. So while she filled out four more bidding slips, I took a long sip of my merlot and focused my attention on the five paintings and the guests bidding on them. From where I was currently standing, I had a view of all five boxes.

While I was waiting, I glanced around the room, noting that pretty much every invitee had a handful of bidding slips in their hands. Spirits were high, and most guests seemed to be having fun, instead of taking it too seriously. Some made a show of trying to look over another's shoulder to see their bids, while others claimed that they were bidding ridiculously high amounts over the reserve price, yet refused to disclose the precise sum.

"Sure, you're doubling the reserve price. You must have sold another book if you're bidding that much," a guest wearing a fur stole and diamond drop earrings countered with a laugh.

"I wish; my agent is still sitting on it," an older man in a monocle and tuxedo replied.

Waiters circled with champagne and three shades of wine, I assumed in the hopes the alcohol would loosen up the bidders and their wallets. And it seemed to be working. Soon cruise ship Gary and the Scottish couple were in a bidding war over the Matisse I was keeping an eye on. Each party laughed as they dropped yet another bid into the box, yet neither seemed content to let the other win.

Yet the way Countess Ursula was acting, making a point of watching the back-and-forth bidding war with a mischievous grin planted on her face, I had a funny feeling she was going to outbid them both for the piece. Sure enough, after both parties had bid a fifth time, Countess Ursula sauntered over and placed her first on the piece. By the way she winked at Gary, we all knew that it was a ridiculously large sum.

Gary and Ursula eyed each other warily until Gary finally grabbed another slip of paper. Apparently Trish had had enough, because she stepped in between them. "I don't know about you, but I could use a beer. Why don't we wait and see who comes out on top, before we bid again, shall we? That's why Cyril's included a second round."

Gary wrapped his arm around his wife's waist. "You're right, doll; let's grab another pint."

After they crossed to the bar, I watched the Italians make a show of bidding on several pieces, but none of the five I was keeping my eye on. The other two investment groups did place bids on the seemingly popular landscape by Cezanne, but they seemed to be randomly selecting which paintings to bid on. Only the Russian had an obvious pattern—he bid on the most expensive ten, which included two of the paintings I was interested in. Apparently his investment portfolio was in good shape.

In fact, other than Rhonda, Countess Ursula was the only one who had slid bids into all five boxes. But then again, Ursula appeared to be bidding on everything.

After much champagne-fueled chitchat, the Baroness did eventually place bids on them, as well. I had not shared the titles with her, leading me to believe that Myrtle had. To what end, I could not tell, seeing as she did not have access to Rosewood's funds. Was it simply to justify her presence at the auction, or was it a subtle hint to me that she knew what was going on, and what was at stake?

I doubted Rhonda had told her, because the Baroness seemed to be ignoring my friend, preferring to hang out with her socialite friends. I didn't mind and in fact hoped her seemingly casual conversations would help us further this case, and maybe garner a new lead or two.

Johnny and his wife had also milled around but not filled out any slips for the first twenty minutes, until he received a message on his phone. Whatever it was put a smile on his face and sent him scurrying around the room, placing bids on several pieces, including one of mine, the portrait by Manet.

His wife, Josie, also developed a sudden interest in that painting, professing loudly that the young girl in it reminded her of their daughter.

Did they have an art consultant? Maybe Johnny had sent him photos of the pieces he was interested in and the expert had finally given him the green light to bid on them. Many private collectors leaned heavily on their art consultant's opinion, especially if they were really only building a collection as an investment.

Considering the lack of attention my five were garnering, Rhonda might just have a chance at winning at least one bid. I could feel a wave of excitement rising up inside of me. If we did manage to win one, it would make it all that much easier to examine the work. With a lot of luck, we might even be able to figure out how Cyril was moving artwork around undetected—as our informant's intel implied.

10

Up the Ante

A few minutes later, Margreta clapped her hands together, after which Cyril called out, "That concludes round one! Margreta will note the highest bids for each painting, and we will make the winners known in a few minutes' time. Good luck."

The pair walked along each of the bid boxes, Margreta with a clipboard in her hand. Cyril lifted each lid and sifted through the slips of paper. Once he'd found the highest bid, he showed it to Margreta so she could write it down, but cupped his hand around it to ensure that none of the guests could see the slip.

"It's really just kitsch, isn't it? But Cyril is a marketing genius, and the story he weaves about bringing back lost art only increases its worth. My art consultant is certain they are only going to grow in value—granted at a slower pace than a painting by the real artist would. That makes putting up with his pompous act worthwhile," Gary was telling another couple, in a voice loud enough for most to hear. Was he trying to bait our host again, or was he simply too tipsy to notice how loudly he was talking?

Trish wasn't taking any chances and shushed him as she pulled him further away from Cyril, leaving me to listen to Rhonda and the Texans chitchat on one side, and the Spanish trio with the Scots on the other. Nothing untoward was being discussed, unfortunately, but rather the joys of living in a desert climate on my right, and the tax benefits of basing your business out of

Ireland, on my left. Which was why I didn't notice Dave coming straight towards me, until he was all up in my personal space.

"Hi Carmen. Did you notice that you have to note which free port you are going to take the art out of? That's a rather odd question, don't you agree?"

My eyes widened as I looked to see who was within earshot. *What is he up to, asking me that kind of question in such a public way?* I wondered. Several guests were standing too close by for my comfort and had cocked their heads towards Dave, as if they were also curious to see where he was going with this.

Dave was treating me like a journalist, not a personal assistant or the friend of someone—my dual roles at this evening's shindig. Was he intentionally trying to get me kicked out of the party?

A sudden and nasty thought set my mind on another path. Or had Rhonda blabbed again and told Dave that I was here undercover and searching for juicy information about our host for the magazine? If she had done that, then there was no way I could recommend her to Reggie as a future agent for the Rosewood Agency.

"I'm just a 'plus-one'; I don't worry my pretty little head about such matters." I did my best to look up at him with a vacant stare.

"Sure." Dave smirked. Yet as he walked past me, he whispered, "Tax evasion. The guy is helping criminals."

I smiled dumbly, but my guard was fully up and my mind on high alert. A typical guest at such an event would know better than to accuse their host of working with criminals, especially when they were standing a few feet away. Whether Dave was a law enforcer or a lawbreaker, my boss needed to know about his comment. I pulled out my phone to ask Myrtle to prioritize his background check, but put it back when Cyril's party planner began clapping again. Once she had everyone's attention, she moved aside and let her boss speak.

"Ladies and gentlemen, it is time to reveal the highest bids! Afterwards, we will open up the gallery again so you have time to view the art once more and reconsider your bids. Margreta, if you please?"

His party planner handed him a sheet of paper, from which he began to read the title of each painting and the highest bid placed so far.

Though he named no names, but only the bidder's number, it was obvious from the guests' pleased or pouty reactions who had won this first round, and who had lost out.

Of my five, the Texans had won the portrait by Manet; the cruise ship couple, the landscape by Cezanne; and Countess Ursula, the Matisse and the Friedrich. Rhonda ended up placing the highest bid for the fifth, the Canaletto I admired—at least for now. By the irritated expressions on many of the guests' faces, I could imagine round two would mean much higher bids. As much as I wanted to celebrate this win, I knew it wasn't a certainty just yet.

"Well, that was a big ole bust. I thought you were going to win more bids, Johnny," Josie grumbled.

"Don't you worry your pretty little head, buttercup. I'll just have to up the ante some more," Johnny said smugly, confirming my suspicions.

Thankfully Reggie had given us room to significantly overbid. At least Serena De Ville had not shown up. From what the other guests had said, she tended to double or even triple the reserve prices. As rich as everyone here was, even they had a limit as to how much "fun money" they were willing to give out on a faux masterpiece.

11

Eyes of a Dragonfly

When Cyril looked at his watch, his irritation was visible. "Margreta, we're running behind schedule. We should have started the second viewing by now. I only have the space reserved for another hour. Make certain you pay better attention to the time."

Margreta bowed her head, but said nothing. My heart went out to her; it had to be a challenge working for such a self-absorbed man.

Cyril looked once again to the entrance, his eyes narrowing as he did. "I suppose Serena was too busy to grace us with her presence. You may be in luck, Johnny."

He slapped the Texan jovially on the back. "Everyone, do keep the highest prices in mind before deciding what to bid the second time around."

"So you really haven't heard from her?" Johnny said as he regarded our host, disbelief evident on his face.

Cyril sighed. "No, I have not. Please, if you will follow me?"

When he led us down the short hallway again, this time I was standing so close to Cyril that I could smell his tangy aftershave, but at least I'd gotten several snaps of the keypad before he shooed me away.

The app I'd purchased and installed without Myrtle or Reggie's knowledge turned my camera's lens into an infrared filter that was supposed to register which keys our host punched to get inside, thanks to the degradation of light and heat within the gel covering the keypad's numbers. Which meant that if everything worked right, I should be able to read the four-digit code he'd used to open the door. It wasn't a perfect system, but because I had taken several photos, it should be easy enough to discern the order in which he had pressed the buttons.

Now that I had acquired the means to enter the gallery later, I was starting to feel pretty good about this job. So I joined Rhonda, now standing in front of the Canaletto.

"Hello, my dear. How are you doing?"

"Great! It's beautiful, isn't it? Say what you want about the man, Cyril can paint. It almost feels like I am looking at a real Canaletto. It calms my soul, just by looking at it, and not much art does that to me. I know I only won the first round, and the chance of winning the second is pretty much zero, but standing here, getting lost in this lovely scene, I have this overwhelming desire to bid my own money on it, so if I did win, I could take it home with me."

I rolled my eyes, instead of chastising her again. As touching as Rhonda's sentiment was, it was not helpful that she had just announced to the room that she was bidding with someone else's money. Instead of talking to Rhonda about being discreet yet again, I decided to ignore her remark. "It is gorgeous. Say, I need to have a quick word with Lady Sophie. Is now a good time?"

In fact, I had a favor to ask of her ladyship, one I believed would make her feel good about coming here tonight.

"Sure, no problem." Rhonda was already lost in the Canaletto again, a slight smile tugging at her lips as she gazed at the painting.

So I glanced around the room until I spotted my partner. Yet before I could reach Sophie, Josie's voice rose up over the din of conversations.

"Golly, it really is the spitting image of Gertrude. Don't you think, Johnny?" Josie said as she stared at a portrait of a young girl, the Manet on my list of stolen items. It was the painting they had won the bid on, at least so far.

Her husband pushed his wide-brimmed hat up and scratched at his forehead. "I didn't see it at first, but now that you mention it, I can't stop seeing our baby girl."

Their sudden and acute interest in the portrait during the first round of bidding had made me take note, but they were the kind of people who probably got obsessed with a work and would bid anything to get their hands on it.

And yet, it was that couple that the framer had accused of knowingly buying stolen artwork. While the Texans did come across as sweet and friendly folks, I knew appearances could deceive. What if they were in on the smuggling operation that Reggie had gotten wind of?

It could have been chance that the framer had singled them out, instead of another couple. But from Johnny's comments, that wasn't the first time Enrico had tried to blackmail them.

Or was the framer simply hoping to blackmail Cyril's clients into paying him to keep his mouth shut—even if his accusations were nothing more than lies? I would have to catch up with Enrico later and interrogate him. Hopefully he would still be angry enough with Cyril to tell me the truth about what our host was doing behind the scenes, as well as who he was working with.

I continued to walk over to the Baroness, making a point of waiting at a discreet distance while she and another lady I didn't recognize gossiped about someone I didn't know. It seemed to go on forever, but probably only a few seconds passed before her conversational partner bid her *adieu*, and her ladyship granted me an audience.

"Carmen, what is there?" Sophie's smile was polite, but her tone was anything but. Given how badly the evening had started, I couldn't fault her for being upset with me.

"I have a job for you."

"Oh really? I thought I was off the clock on this one because your darling friend is here to save the day." The corners of her mouth rose up, but her tone was as sharp as a knife.

"I was hoping you could help me wheedle a bit of information out of Ursula, but if you don't want to, I can send Rhonda in."

My words worked like a charm. "Oh, no—Rhonda is not going to offend another friend of mine."

I had to suppress a chuckle at her word choice. Before this evening began, the Baroness would have told anyone who'd listen about what a horrid person Countess Ursula was. But at this party they were on the same social rung, one that was much higher than mine or Rhonda's, despite my friend's bulging bank account.

"That's what I figured you'd say. She won the bids on two of the pieces I'm keeping an eye on. Can you find out why she is interested in those two particular paintings?"

"Certainly," she said, in casual acknowledgement—without winking or staring at Countess Ursula, as Rhonda would have done.

If only my bestie could be so subtle. I had to admit that while I enjoyed having her by my side, Rhonda was not really cut out to be an undercover sleuth of any kind. I'd have to talk to Reggie about that, in case he was still considering offering her a position.

Now that the matter with Ursula was settled, I turned my attention back to the artwork. Margreta was busy adding stickers with the current highest bid to each description board. *Smart move*, I thought.

Yet I was not interested in their value, but in trying to discern who was telling the truth—the framer or Cyril. I checked my phone, but Myrtle had not yet responded to my request for more information on the confiscated paintings. So I messaged her, hoping to push her into action. "Any news on the art's authenticity? Picking up signals that they are possibly fakes."

I was feeling deflated that I had discovered so little and that I remained uncertain about what was really going on. Without examining the paintings, I wasn't going to get much further with this assignment. But until I could get some alone time with the art, I had another source I could lean on—my best friend. However, before I conferred with Rhonda, I wanted to send the framer's name to Myrtle, so she could check into his background.

Since he had been ejected from the party, I would have to ask the party planner about him. When I spotted Margreta checking her phone, I rushed over, in the hopes of speaking to her alone.

"Excuse me, but do you know the name of the angry young man who was causing trouble earlier and got escorted out? I believe his first name is Enrico."

"Who?" was her confused response to what I had assumed was a simple-to-answer question. After a moment's hesitation, her face brightened. "Oh, yes, you mean Enrico Greco. He works—or should say worked—as a framer at Cyril's gallery. It's odd, he was one of Cyril's favorites because he did such great work. That's why he asked Enrico to help out with the auction, after one of the other framers fell ill."

"Do you know why Enrico was so upset? He was making some pretty wild accusations about Cyril smuggling art."

Margreta shook her head. "I really do not know why he was lashing out like that, or telling all of those horrid lies. But then, these auctions are always quite chaotic because everything has to happen at the last minute. Maybe the stress of it all got to him and made him see things that weren't there."

She bit her lip and glanced over at the Italian art dealer, busy chatting up two socialites who were young enough to be his daughters. "Enrico worked for Manzino first, before he moved up to Luxembourg a few years ago."

I followed her eyeline and leaned in closer. "Do more of Cyril's staff come from Manzino?"

"Not many. He's sent up a few framers and copy artists that wanted to live in northern Europe for a while, but none lasted long. They are too proud for Cyril's liking. Enrico was the only exception."

"Interesting, thank you."

"Sure, no problem." When she looked down at her phone again, I knew that I was already forgotten.

I grabbed my own mobile and ticked Enrico's name into a message for Myrtle, sending it off before I sought my friend. If the framer had a criminal record or any prior convictions, my company contact would find it.

It was now time to corner my bestie and pick her brain. She was chatting with the Texan couple, laughing and joking as if they were old friends. I stood far enough away to not catch their attention, but near enough to be in her sightline. When she noticed me, I jerked my head to one side, signaling for her to join me, away from the Bighorns.

Moments later, Rhonda strolled over to me before asking in a shy voice, "How did your conversation with Lady Sophie go?"

"Fine. I asked her to find out why Countess Ursula is interested in a particular painting and know Lady Sophie will be able to wheedle it out of her. They aren't friends, but are often allies."

Rhonda's face brightened up. "It sure is a good thing that she's here."

I looked sideways at my friend, but there was no snideness in her voice or expression. "Yes, it is. It's great to have you here helping me with the bidding, and to have her here to interrogate all of the royals swarming around."

"So, Rhonda…" I leaned in as close as I dared and whispered, "If you were smuggling art out of the country, how would you do it? I'm looking for a professional guess, but I am not going to include anything you say in the article," I soothed, hoping she would be completely candid with me.

Rhonda looked to the painting in front of us, a lovely landscape originally by Caspar David Friedrich. "I've been wondering the same thing. He would have been a fool to paint over the whole thing, so I'm going to discount that theory straight away."

She nodded towards the wide black frame surrounding the painting in front of us. "Several of the frames are quite wide, but none appear to be broad or deep enough to hide another rolled-up canvas inside of."

I nodded encouragingly, glad she'd already discounted two of my theories and for the same reasons that I had.

When she suddenly leaned back on one heel and tapped a finger on her chin, my spirits rose even further. An idea must have popped into her brain. So I waited patiently for it to take form, studying the canvas to see whether I could see what she did.

When she spoke, moments later, I had high hopes she was onto something. "Could he have mounted the real one behind his copy? That would be a perfect way to smuggle an original out of the country."

A sigh escaped my lips. I had already had the same thought, but dismissed it after seeing the back. "It would be, but it's not how he's doing it. Cyril took one off of the wall earlier, and the back was clearly a new canvas, unpainted except for his signature. So no, the originals are not mounted behind his copy."

Rhonda blew out her cheeks. "I must say, I was hoping it would be a little more obvious. But then, you did say that this smuggling ring has been operating for quite some time. It's probably exceedingly simple, but I am at a loss as to how. Unless…"

The next thing I knew, she was knocking on Cyril's copy of Friedrich's work as if it was a door. "That's odd," she said with a frown.

I grabbed her shoulders and jerked her away from the canvas, hoping no one had seen what she'd done. Had she not heard what I'd said about the back being new?

Cyril had thankfully not seen her action, but another guest had and was rolling her way towards us at top speed.

"What are you doing?" the Baroness seethed as soon as she was within hearing range. "You seemed so normal when I met you last. Why are you acting like a clown? You are putting my reputation on the line—behave yourself!"

"Whoa, let's take it down a notch, Lady Sophie. Rhonda is not a fool or a child." They had only met once before, and it had been delightful seeing them chat as if they were old acquaintances, instead of strangers. Which is why I had not expected that Sophie would act so callously towards my friend, even if Rhonda had clearly messed up.

"Rhonda, can you try not to do anything that could offend our host again? It's embarrassing enough that you are my guest. Try to respect the fact that Cyril considers himself an artist. He would be livid if he'd seen what you had done."

My friend's head was already drooping, but Sophie continued her onslaught.

"These may not be genuine masterpieces by Gauguin and Cezanne, but our host considers them to be. Don't treat them like your collectibles, but as fine art. Would you knock on a Matisse in a museum?"

"No, and I would be mad if I saw someone else doing so. There was just something off about the texture and sound," Rhonda admitted, obviously dismayed that she'd upset the Baroness. "But that doesn't give me the right to act a fool. I should apologize to our host."

"No!" the Baroness practically screamed, her fingers clamping around

Rhonda's wrist like a vise. "Please leave Cyril be. He's in a particularly fragile mood. He and Manzino are in a disagreement about something that has him quite upset. Which is poor timing on the Italian's part. Cyril only holds these auctions once a year; you would think that he would have had the decency to wait to talk to Cyril about whatever is bothering him, until after the auction."

"Well, I did overhear a smidgen of their conversation and know that whatever it is, Cyril has been avoiding talking to Manzino about it, which is why he crashed this party." It was a slight risk talking shop with the Baroness like this in front of Rhonda, but hopefully my friend would only think that we were gossiping about the host and guests.

"That makes so much more sense." The Baroness was quiet a moment, before adding, "Still, let's give Cyril space and mingle instead. Perhaps we'll overhear something useful."

12

The Diva Arrives

Before Rhonda or I could respond, the door to the gallery burst open. "Hello, everyone! The queen of the party has arrived—let the fun begin!"

In the doorway stood an apparition in silk and chiffon. A tall, mocha-skinned woman, dressed in flowing robes and silk scarves that Stevie Nicks would adore, floated into the room. I recognized her immediately, as did pretty much everyone in the room, I suspected. The former supermodel and the current owner of the De Ville Agency—one of the world's most successful modeling agencies—was hard to miss. She had been the first African-American model to grace the cover of all of the important fashion magazines, and now her company was regularly featured in the more popular lifestyle and business publications.

Trailing behind her was a preppy-looking young man dressed to the nines. His Prada shoes were polished so highly, the lights reflected off of their surface with each step.

"Shucks, I thought we had a shot at cleaning house this time. I guess we'll have to up the ante quite a bit if we want to take anything home," Johnny grumbled to Josie.

"And I thought I had a chance at that Cezanne," Gary moaned to Trish.

The way the three investor groups were gesturing towards Serena and talking in rapid, yet hushed, tones led me to believe they were thinking the same thing.

"Serena, my dear. How kind of you to grace us with your presence." Cyril's tone was light and airy, but his expression was dark and brooding.

"We arrived much later than expected thanks to someone's inability to hurry up," Serena's companion replied as he glanced over at his date—whose makeup, hair, and clothes were catwalk ready. "Now we missed our chance to get a good look at the artwork, as well as the first round of bidding. You know how I love to gamble."

By the way he stuck out his lower lip as he spoke, I could already tell that I was not going to like this privileged young man.

"And it was worth every second—I look fabulous." When Serena patted her hair, the emerald, sapphire, and ruby rings covering her fingers caught the light, and for a moment, her hand seemed to light up like a Christmas tree.

"Is that her latest boy toy?" another heavily bejeweled woman whispered.

"They change every time," her snarky companion replied.

"There was no reason for you to rush over, if you weren't really interested in purchasing my artwork. I should warn you that we are about to conclude this second viewing and start the last round of bidding. We do have a schedule to maintain. You may want to bow out on this auction."

Instead of being gracious and welcoming, Cyril almost seemed mad that she had bothered to show up. That was odd to me, considering earlier this evening, he seemed to be eagerly anticipating her arrival.

"Don't be silly. I adore your repeats and can't wait to decorate my Italian palazzo with more of them. Besides, I know what I want when I see it. It's not like I plan on meditating over the purchase first. We will still have time to bid on everything I desire."

By the way he clenched his jaw, I had a feeling Cyril would prefer that she leave, but that he didn't dare try to eject her or forbid her from taking part in the auction.

After a moment's hesitation, he turned to address the room. "Alright, dear guests. You have fifteen more minutes before we begin the second round of bidding."

That was enough to stop the general chitchat as the invitees turned to examine Cyril's copies one last time. When Serena and her companion passed by the Baroness, Sophie called out, "Where did you find this one? He must be half your age."

Serena slowed her gait to take in my partner's fractured foot and wheelchair. "Oh, hi Sophie. We met at a club, and yes, he is."

She smiled wickedly as she patted her friend's backside, before adding in a bored tone. "What happened to you, anyway? Oh, never mind, I really don't care."

Serena turned to her companion, just in time to miss the look of shock that crossed the Baroness's face. "Bobby, Sophie is a baroness. Why don't you be a good boy and introduce yourself properly. I need to talk to Cyril. Ciao."

Despite her condescending tone, Bobby dutifully turned to Sophie and held out his hand. "Hello, I'm Baron Robert Maria Otto Balthus Riddell. Where does your family hail from?"

Why did royals always have such long names? I wondered. Probably so it was easier to trace each other's lineage through those unique combinations of first and middle names. And they always asked about each other's ancestry, as if it was important to know whether their distant relatives were connected in some way.

"Roxburghshire, in southern Scotland."

The Baron's face lit up. "Isn't that a gas—so are we. Which line are you?"

Sophie began to cough into her fist, as if she was choking on an invisible drink. But I knew her well enough to see through her coughing fit. The Baron had upset her in some way, and she was taking a moment to compose herself. "The Rutherfords."

I knew the region was small, as was the chance that we would run into someone hailing from the same area, but I didn't understand why this coincidence seemed to have upset Sophie so. Was she simply embarrassed that her ancestors had once lived in the same region as Bobby's family?

The Baron frowned. "Oh, I thought that line died out."

My partner added softly, "We did lose our land three generations ago. That must be what you are thinking of."

The Baron squinted at her, and for a moment it seemed as if he wanted to say something more, but ultimately he held his tongue. Instead of engaging with her further, he began looking around the room for another conversational partner.

The Baroness blushed slightly at the dis and did the same. I had a feeling the two would ignore each other for the rest of the party, though I still didn't understand why either was acting as they were.

Seconds later, my partner snapped her fingers, presumably to get her nurse's attention, then pointed towards the door. "Please take me to the bar. I would like a glass of chardonnay."

Her matronly nurse complied, pushing her patient out of the gallery and back towards the lounge without a word.

I looked around for Rhonda, just as Margreta clapped her hands together again. "Ladies and gentlemen, it is time to commence the second round of bidding."

13

Second Round of Bidding

Soon after we were herded back into the dining area, my partner waved me over to the bar. "I'm afraid the chardonnay did not agree with me. I'm feeling rather woozy, and I would prefer to return to the hotel."

"Of course. Can I help with anything?"

"No, it's all been taken care of. Could you perhaps stop by my hotel room, after you're finished here?"

"Certainly. Although I do hope you will be asleep by then."

"That sounds reasonable. Whatever happens, I expect you to catch me up either later tonight or tomorrow."

"You got it, partner."

The Baroness squeezed my hand ever so briefly, then signaled for her nurse to get them out of there.

When I noted Rhonda watching my partner roll away, I popped over to let her know what was going on.

"Oh, that's too bad that's she's feeling so poorly. But I still can't believe she actually came here, considering she is in so much pain."

"Me either," I said ruefully. "She didn't think it through, I'm afraid."

"Still, it's a good thing she did show up, otherwise Cyril would have kicked us out," Rhonda said, echoing my partner's earlier remarks.

I gave my friend a quick hug. There were so many things that I loved about her, including her ability to admit fault and move on.

"Could you please bid on the same five paintings again, but this time go twenty thousand over the highest bid placed so far? Let's see if we can get ahold of at least one of them."

Rhonda shook her hands out in front of her, as if they were wet. "Oh la la—I'm sure glad it's not my money! But I'm happy to play along."

"And while you are doing that, I'm going to disappear for a bit. If anyone asks, could you say that I'm in the restroom?"

"You got it!" Rhonda squeezed my shoulder before setting off to grab more bidding slips. As long as she didn't tell the Texans that I had told her to bid on those five paintings, everything would work out alright. At least I had to assume it would, because now was probably my only chance to sneak off to the gallery.

I excused myself and rushed off to the bathroom, looking as uncomfortable as I could, in the hopes that any others considering using the facilities would grant me a little privacy. As soon as the stall door closed, I pulled out my phone and examined the photos I'd made of the keypad.

Several were slightly blurred, but that didn't really matter. It was the color that I cared about. The infrared filter captured whatever numbers Cyril had pushed, his touch turning the normally greenish-glow of the keypad into flames of oranges and reds. Thanks to the rapid degradation of temperature, I could even tell the order. The first two numbers were clear—5 and 7—but Johnny's hat had blocked the third push. Luckily by the time Cyril pushed in the fourth number—2—it was lit up bright red. Meaning the orangey key—number 4—must have been the third button he had pushed in.

There was only one way to find out whether I had gotten it right, and no time to second-guess myself. If I wasn't quick, Margreta would surely come looking for me. I cracked the bathroom door open and saw no one in the hallway, so I stepped out and rushed over to the gallery door, walking as softly as I could in my thick-heeled pumps.

As soon as I pushed in 5-7-4-2, the door opened with a soft click. I was feeling pretty good about how easy it was to break in, but knew I only had a few minutes to study Cyril's work, before my presence would be missed. So I suppressed the urge to pump my arm in celebration and instead walked straight over to the first stolen painting I spotted and pulled it down. Thanks to Cyril's earlier demonstration, I didn't need to worry about the painting being secured to the wire or protected by motion detectors.

Just as I turned it over to examine the back and frame for any clues, a terse voice made me freeze instantly.

"Put that back."

I held onto the painting tight, until a familiar face stepped out of the shadows. Only when the frame began to slip through my fingers did I realize that my grip had slackened, as had my jaw.

"Dave? What are you doing here—trying to give me a heart attack?"

"I said, hang the painting back up."

I stared down at the painting in my hands, as if I had no idea how it had gotten there. "Oh, this thing? Yeah, um, it's not what it looks like?"

Dave leaned back on one heel and crossed his arms over his torso. "Sure, you just wanted to get a better look at it, right?"

I glared up at him. "Hey, you aren't supposed to be in here, either. So why are you?"

"For the same reason as you, Carmen De Luca—art sleuth for the Rosewood Agency."

That caught my attention. The chances were slim that he had pulled my profession out of thin air. Did someone blab, or did he find a connection online? Whatever the reason, I chose to play dumb. "The what-now agency?"

He sighed as his fingers began drumming on one well-formed bicep. "Cute. I know all about you, Carmen. After you'd arranged with the French police for Harold Moreau's Book of Hours to be returned to a museum in Ohio, I had my organization run a background check on you. You were one of Rosewood's senior sleuths until a personal tragedy sent you into early retirement, more than three years ago. Yet for some reason, you recently partnered back up with Baroness Rutherford, and the two of you have been searching for stolen art ever since."

I sucked in my breath, refusing to let my emotions get the best of me. It was hard to stay dry-eyed when my husband, Carlos, entered the conversation, however briefly. But it was eerie to hear how much Dave had already learned about me. Could he be a private detective, or an operative for one of the many governmental organizations known by a three-letter acronym? "It sounds like you've done your homework. And who exactly do you work for?"

"Interpol, the Fine Arts Division. Dave Swanson, good to meet you." He held out a hand.

When I began to lower the painting to the floor, so that I could shake it, he suddenly held up both palms, as if to stop me. "Can you put the painting back first? There is a tracker on the frame, and I don't want you accidentally knocking it out of place."

"Really?" I examined the surface, my professional curiosity piqued. I wished Reggie would allow me to use trackers and homing devices, but he was always more focused on my not breaking international laws than in considering what the gear could gain us in intel.

"Yep, it's that semitransparent sticker on the edge of the frame." When he pointed to the tracker, a clear decal half the size of a postage stamp, I couldn't help but be envious. If he hadn't pointed it out, I never would have noticed it.

"See it there? I just finished placing it, so the glue has probably not set yet. Please be careful with that."

"Alright already." As gently as I could, I replaced the painting on the wire and backed up a step, to make sure it was hanging correctly. "Happy now?"

"Yes, ecstatic."

"So, do tell. Why is Interpol interested in Cyril Bouve?"

"For reasons similar to those of the Rosewood Agency, I bet."

I folded my arms over my chest and leaned back on one heel, mimicking his posture. "You first."

"Okay. Technically, I'm here as part of the Incident Response Team, deployed at Italy's request to offer expertise and investigative support on a new lead they are following up. One that involves Cyril Bouve and Nico Manzino."

When he paused and raised an eyebrow at me, I shook my head. That was not enough information to satisfy me. "And what new lead is that?"

His eyes narrowed as he studied me, as if he wasn't certain that he could trust me.

"You unmasked me, remember? I don't know you from Adam."

He held his ground for a moment, until I jutted out my chin and began tapping my foot.

"Fine. So, we suspect tax evasion and whitewashing for criminal organizations. There might even be a little forgery going on."

I couldn't help but chuckle. "That sounds like quite a smorgasbord of crimes."

"Yeah, well, they may all be intertwined. We suspect Cyril of tax evasion because of the values he's set on his artwork sold during this auction. Owners are allowed to sell their art within the confines of a free port without notifying the tax authorities, as long as the sale is under one hundred thousand dollars. And the person who brings the work into the free port self-discloses the value, which leaves plenty of room for undervaluing an object."

"Okay, so you think Cyril is going to lie about the amount paid for these pieces? That makes sense. So far, several of the bids have been over one hundred thousand dollars. So why do you suspect whitewashing?"

I was getting a little impatient. We didn't have much time to examine the artwork, but I didn't feel comfortable doing my job in front of this person quite yet. I did have my own theories, but wanted to hear his first. Reggie Rosewood had been so focused on catching Cyril in the act of doing something illicit, he hadn't yet sought how that artist's actions could fit into the bigger scheme of things. Dave and Interpol were focused on the entire network of criminals. We really were working the same case, yet from two different angles.

"My Italian colleagues are more interested in Nico Manzino than Cyril because several of the sales made through his gallery are suspicious. That's why the Italians requested Interpol's assistance. The prices are far too high for what he is selling, which in and of itself is not so strange. But in most cases, the buyers used falsified paperwork to purchase them, leaving us with no trail to follow and no way to obtain hard evidence. In a few other cases, we believe he sold artwork he knew to be stolen and helped to ensure that those buyers could not be traced, either. He's a slippery character, as are his clients, it seems."

My eyebrows knitted together. Maybe we weren't really working the same case, after all. "So where do you get whitewashing from and how does Cyril Bouve fit in?"

"These annual auctions were traditionally held in Nico's gallery in Venice, and several pieces sold through his gallery were also recovered in various raids on criminals' homes over the past few months. Informants have also told us about certain stolen pieces of art being used in criminal transactions and their sales being brokered by Nico. Yet some of the recovered paintings were the genuine articles, while others were well-made copies."

I nodded. "And you suspect the copies were painted by Cyril."

"We do. Since he ships so much artwork down to Nico, everything he's sold through the Italian is now suspect. Cyril certainly has the talent, and it sounds like Nico has the connections. But honestly, it's all gotten so muddled, it's hard to know where one crime begins and another ends. Nor do we know who all the players are. Which is why my boss wants me to keep it simple and try to get Cyril for tax evasion. All I have to do is prove he has sold artwork for more than one hundred thousand, and I've got him."

"Sexy."

"Yeah, well, the FBI started it when they got Al Capone for tax evasion. It may not be sensational, but it gets the job done."

"Fair enough."

"So you aren't here for the whitewashing or tax evasion, but for the smuggling?" Dave asked, clearly seeking confirmation.

"That's right. We suspect Cyril Bouve is making copies of stolen art and may be smuggling both the original and his copy down to Italy via this annual auction. But to what end, or for whom, we do not yet know. Which is why I'm here. No one at the Rosewood Agency is aware of the whitewashing or tax angle, so far as I know."

Dave nodded enthusiastically, "Excellent information; thanks for sharing. It's clear they are up to something, which is why I've placed trackers on all of the frames. Hopefully they'll stay on long enough for us to figure out where the artwork goes after it leaves the Luxembourg free port."

"You don't need to bother tracking them all. According to our intel, there are only five we should be concerned with." I explained that they were the only ones not stolen during World War II and showed him Reggie's message, figuring I might as well start off our cooperation on the right foot.

"Interesting; now we can both narrow our focus," Dave mused, then turned to study the piece I'd just hung back up. "So you think he's painted over the original? Like they did with the Van Goghs during the war?"

I ran my fingers lightly over the top layer before pushing my fingernail into a tiny drip of paint that was a bit thicker than the rest. My nail left a clear mark in the soft paint. "You're referring to the Vincent Van Gogh paintings that were painted over, and thereby saved from destruction, during WWII. But that was a totally different situation. And if Cyril did try to do that, he was a little too liberal with the oils. Did you see how thick the top layer of paint is? It would be a nightmare to remove all of that, and the damage to the original would render it worthless."

Dave examined it again for a few moments. "They are the best fakes I've ever seen; even the craquelure is realistic."

"They are repeats—not fakes," I said, mimicking Cyril's snooty voice.

When I ran my hand over the framed edge, Dave gave me a plaintive look. "I hate to break it to you, but I already examined the frames when I was placing the trackers and didn't see any spaces large enough to hold another work."

I sighed. "I figured as much. And they aren't double-framed because the back of the canvas is new."

"Maybe there's a hidden panel in the transportation crate."

I nodded. "That's a good one. He could have used the same method to get it into the free port, so the customs officers think there is only one painting, not two. We should look at the crates, if we can find them."

"Excellent idea," Dave said as he checked his watch. "Shoot, we've been gone for ten minutes. The crates are going to have to wait. I think we should head back before the bidding ends."

"I agree." I hoped Rhonda had already placed her bids on all five, but did want to check that she'd done so, before it was too late.

I started towards the door when Dave said, "Before we do, you should know that we believe that Cyril has one or two ringers in the audience tonight, to ensure that certain paintings are shipped to the free port in Trieste, Italy. Do you have any ideas as to who it might be?"

I racked my mind for the answer, but it was hard to do while staring into Dave's gorgeous blue eyes. I didn't really have anything solid on Countess Ursula or Serena to share, only a gut feeling that one or both may be involved. "Nothing concrete yet. I've been watching to see who bids on the five paintings. I figure if there is an accomplice, he or she will do whatever it takes to win those bids."

Dave nodded in appreciation. "That's great. I'll be curious to see who ends up with them."

As we walked to the door, a sudden thought made me pause. "Say, I used an infrared filter to puzzle out the keycode. How did you get in?"

He pulled a gizmo out of his pocket that wasn't much bigger than a cell phone. "This little baby can unlock any electronic lock within a matter of seconds."

I regarded it with envy, knowing my boss would never allow me to carry around something so obviously criminal.

"Nice. Maybe, if the chance presents itself, you'd let me try it out sometime."

Dave's face brightened up. "Sure thing."

14

The Winner Is

"One last thing," Dave said, his hand on the gallery door's handle. "When I saw you arrive, I called my boss to let him know about Rosewood being on the job. We'd had a few incidents with your agency in the past, when we were working the same cases but didn't share intel, and I wanted to avoid repeating that mistake."

I nodded, recalling Sophie mentioning something similar, a few weeks ago.

Dave cleared his throat and looked to his shoe. "He subsequently got in touch with your boss, Reginald Rosewood, who agreed to assign you to me."

"Say what? I'm not a piece of meat, you know." The way he said it made me sound like an object that could be tossed around. That kind of talk always made my blood boil.

"Technically, I am the lead on this case, but I consider you to be my equal. I was hoping we could share information, regardless of our titles. I don't need the credit, but I would like to see at least Manzino put behind bars by the end of this mission. Would you help me figure out what he and Cyril are up to?"

I regarded my so-called boss. As much as I wanted to be mad at Dave for this turn of events, I would have done the same and called my superior, had I known he was Interpol. Besides, there was a real chance that by working together, we could wrap up this case faster than if I was working alone. So instead of getting even madder, I looked up at him, my voice and expression as sincere as could be.

"You had me at 'links to a criminal organization.' But I do want to check in with my boss before saying yes."

"No problem, I would want to do the same."

Dave held the door open for me. Just as he closed the gallery door behind us, the sound of another door opening farther up the hallway set us both on edge. I pushed myself into the gallery's doorway, but it was way too narrow to hide me, let alone both of us. I frantically searched for another hiding place, but there was none. Besides, it was already too late. Bearing down on us at top speed was Cyril's assistant.

Margreta gasped when she noted that Dave and I were standing just outside the gallery. "What are you doing here?"

I began to stammer a response when Dave wrapped one hand around my neck and pulled me in for a long kiss, as if he hadn't noticed or heard Margreta—but only had eyes for me.

I knew he was just using the old "drunken lovers making out in the hallway" trick, to give us a valid reason for stepping away from the party, but his kiss was electric, and for a moment, I reveled in his touch.

Margreta had to clear her throat twice before we pulled apart. "Excuse me, there are only a few more minutes left to bid before we announce the winners. You were planning on bidding again, weren't you, Mr. Swanson?"

It was much more difficult to leave his warm embrace than I'd expected it to be. I filed that sensation and his kiss away, to mull over later.

"Oh, hi, Margreta." I kept my eyes downcast and straightened my dragonfly brooch, the fitting response for a woman embarrassed at being caught out.

Dave grinned as he wrapped an arm around my waist. "You'll have to excuse me; we haven't seen each other in while. This lady sure does get my blood boiling."

I blushed as I took his hand and pulled it off of my hip, all the while keeping my eyes averted. "Sorry about that."

"I've already placed my bids, but am curious to see if I've won any of them. I hope Serena or Johnny didn't overbid on everything," Dave gushed, a little too enthusiastically. His cheeks were flushed, I noted, glad that our kiss hadn't left him indifferent.

"We'll all find out who won the bids in just a few minutes," Margreta replied tersely, before she turned on her heel and rushed down the hallway, obviously in a hurry to get back to the auction and her demanding boss.

We trailed behind slowly, my fingers still clasped around his. Holding hands probably wasn't necessary, but it did fit in with our new cover story, and in all honesty, it felt pretty darn good.

Before we reached the lounge, my phone pinged. I pulled it out with my free hand and saw that it was a new message from Reggie asking me to call when I could. I had a pretty good idea of what he wanted to tell me. I considered popping into the bathroom to call him back and let him know that I'd already talked to Dave, but Margreta was expecting us to return to the auction. My boss would have to wait until I was back at the hotel.

When we entered the lounge, the room was abuzz with nervous chatter and lots of loud whispering. Margreta was already by Cyril's side, helping to tally up the bids, their heads close together to ensure no one else heard what they were discussing. At least until the Swedes interrupted and asked to speak to Cyril about another matter—a commission that he was late delivering. When he pulled them aside, his assistant continued on her own.

Standing by the bidding box for the Manet portrait were the Bighorns and Serena De Ville.

"I just know we're going to win that portrait. I can feel it in my bones," Josie said in a voice loud enough to ensure everyone heard her.

"Are you so certain?" Serena, the archenemy among the collectors, replied in the sweetest of voices. "I bid on it, too. I suppose we'll find out in a moment who actually won."

The smugness in her tone told me the Texans were probably out of luck. By the way their bodies deflated with her every word, it looked as if they agreed with me.

The portrait was one of the five on my list. Was it a coincidence that both parties were so interested in it? Or was Serena simply pestering the Texans? They did seem to have a history.

The idea that she could be the ringer that Dave had mentioned flittered through my brain. Yet Cyril wasn't exactly pleased to see her when she finally did arrive—practically at the end of the auction. I tapped my chin, thinking back to how Cyril was expecting her to show up much earlier, and when he finally realized that she may not grace us with her presence, he had pulled Countess Ursula aside. But Ursula seemed to have bid on everything during the first round, not just those five. Maybe Dave was wrong, and there was no ringer.

Unfortunately, now was not the time to discuss my suspicions with him; the room was simply too crowded. So I looked around for Rhonda, hoping she had in fact bid again. When I finally made eye contact, she had apparently already spotted us. Strangely, her eyes were fixated on my hands, and her mouth was already transforming into a large O.

"Shoot!" I muttered and dropped Dave's hand. Rhonda was never going to let this go now. She was convinced that I needed to find a new man to share my life with. I knew she had loved her husband as much as I did mine, and that it was healthy to move on, as she'd done, but I just wasn't ready to do so. One day, I hoped to be. But there was still a part of me that expected Carlos to come home every night, even though I knew he was gone forever. It was as if my soul couldn't accept he was really dead and could still feel his presence here on our physical plane.

I shook the thought loose, knowing my feelings were normal after a person's partner died so unexpectedly.

Luckily, before Rhonda could reach Dave or me, Cyril grabbed ahold of the clipboard in Margreta's hands and moved into the center of the room.

There were lots of smug looks and nervous glances as the artist and auctioneer glanced over the bidding sheets. Yet his frown increased dramatically the longer he looked. By the time he'd reached the end, he looked positively stricken. "Is this a mistake, Margreta?"

His assistant shook her head and glared at Serena. "No, sir."

Cyril held the clipboard to his chest. "Ladies and gentlemen, let me have a quick word with Miss De Ville before we proceed."

Our host grabbed the former model's elbow and moved her over to one side of the room. Yet it was small enough that everyone could easily hear what they were discussing.

"What are you doing?"

"What you asked me to do," Serena purred back.

Cyril pulled away from her and stared at her wide-eyed, as if she was crazy. "I have no idea what you are talking about. I didn't ask you to do anything. Regardless, I must say that what you have done tonight is unacceptable."

Serena's head flew back as her cackle filled the room. "Why not?"

"Either share, or you won't be invited again," Cyril demanded.

Serena pouted but finally nodded. "Fine, be boring."

Cyril cleared his throat as he stepped back into the center of the space. "Ladies and gentlemen, it seems one person has won all of the bids—our late arrival." He gestured towards Serena as the rest began to grumble.

"Why bother arranging an auction if you are going to sell everything to one buyer?" Trish moaned.

"That was never my intention," Cyril asserted.

Serena ticked her tongue against her teeth. "Crybabies. I guess I'm more of a fan of Cyril's work than you are. Regardless, I'll withdraw my bid on several, but not all, mind you." She wagged a manicured finger at the others. "And I get to choose."

She sauntered over to Cyril and pointed out the paintings she still wished to bid on, before stepping over to the bar.

Cyril waited until she'd ordered a drink, before continuing. "Alright, we will ignore Serena's bid on the remaining paintings, and the second-highest bidder will be considered the winner. Is that acceptable?"

"Definitely," the Scottish man called out.

"Let's just get this show on the road—I want my portrait!" Josie said, getting a laugh out of the rest.

As Cyril broadcast the names of the winners, the invitees' smug and jittery responses to each announcement made clear which guests had gotten what they wanted, and which had lost out. I began to mentally note who won what, until I recalled that only five mattered.

Which was how I came to realize that Serena had rescinded her bid on all of the paintings—save the five I was after. Was she Cyril's ringer, after all? Maybe that whole disagreement about the bids was an act. I would have to see which free port she had written down as the painting's final delivery destination. If it was Italy, I would say that Dave and I had found Cyril's partner in crime.

After Cyril had declared Serena the new owner of the five paintings I was interested in, Miss De Ville began to prance around the room, rubbing her win in pretty much everyone's faces. It turned out that several guests had set their hearts on one or more of them.

Based on her pouty reaction to Serena's dance of joy, Countess Ursula was one of the sore losers. Yet her disappointment didn't feel genuine to me, but more of a show for the others.

My new Interpol friend did win one bid, though not on any of the five stolen pieces, unfortunately. However, he did list Trieste as its final destination, which I thought was clever. He said it was because he was on his way to Venice to meet his client, a rich Italian recluse who collected Cyril's lost paintings because her own family had lost so many during the war—an excellent cover story, in my opinion.

But the biggest and loudest losers were Rhonda's buddies, the Bighorns. After Cyril announced that Serena had won the portrait the Texans were obsessed with, a cry of disbelief rose up from the pair.

Cruise ship Gary was also pretty vocal about losing out to Miss De Ville on one of the stolen paintings. "How could you have possibly won? I bid seventy-five thousand dollars on that landscape, and the reserve price was fifty thousand. How much did you bid?"

"I bid twice the reserve price," Serena said, smiling when Gary's jaw dropped. "If you really wanted that Cezanne, you should have bid more."

"Well, that means we did win that Manet portrait fair and square—we bid triple the reserve price, not double," Johnny announced, causing several partygoers to gasp, presumably as they pondered his ridiculously high bid.

The reserve price for the Manet was also fifty grand, meaning he'd paid a whopping one hundred and fifty dollars for that copy. My heart skipped a beat; that meant Dave now had the proof he needed to demonstrate Cyril was trying to evade the tax authorities. At least, if Cyril lied about the final bid amount on the customs forms.

Margreta took a moment to check the clipboard Cyril had already handed back to her. "Are you certain, sir? I see Serena's bid is the highest one, at one hundred thousand dollars."

"Are you calling me a liar, little lady?" When Johnny pushed up the brim of his hat, I could see his eyes were narrowing to slits.

Cyril's assistant straightened up and pushed her glasses back up her nose, making clear that she would not be intimidated. "No, sir. All I am saying is that Serena's bid appears to be the highest one placed in the bidding box."

"That can't be right. Is there a hole in that box?" Johnny growled as he leaned in on our host.

Cyril held up his hands and waved the Texan back out of his personal space. Only after Johnny had taken a large step backwards did Cyril straighten his scarf and clear his throat. "You won two of the bids, one of which our Russian friend really wanted to purchase—is that not true, Vladimir? I would say that you did quite well tonight."

"But Johnny, that little girl looks just like Gertrude," Josie whined.

"I don't care what you think; my wife wants that portrait, and I'm not leaving here until I get it. We did put in the winning bid, despite what your clipboard says. If you aren't going to be man enough to double-check the bid box, then I will."

When the Texan lunged for the box, Cyril grabbed ahold of it first and held it close to his chest. But Johnny was a bull with his sights on red. The much larger man easily pulled the small box out of Cyril's hands and tore off the wooden lid. When he did, a folded slip of paper fluttered to the ground, as if it had been stuck between the lid and the side of the box.

Johnny tore it open and held it up for all to see. "What did I tell you? My bid was higher than Serena's. I finally got you, girl! This one's going home with us."

When Johnny pulled his wife in for a long kiss, Cyril began to shake his head, as if he couldn't process what had just occurred. "I have never had such a situation before. I assure you, it was a horrible oversight. Margreta—look what you did! You missed a bid, and the winning one, at that."

His party planner looked up at him with so much confusion on her face, it was clear to all that she had no idea what he was talking about. Yet, as any dedicated assistant would, she said nothing, but instead let his insults roll off of her back.

"I can't wait to take this home and show it to Gertrude. Can we take it back to the hotel with us now?" Josie pleaded. "I could look at her all night."

When Cyril looked to his watch, his eyebrows knitted together. "Oh, bother. It is quite a bit of paperwork, and I'm afraid I'm a little light in the head. Besides, I want to offer everyone a nightcap back at the hotel's bar. Could we start the process in the morning?"

Johnny eyed him suspiciously, but ultimately a grin spread over his face. "Sure, partner. First thing in the morning, alright?"

"Certainly. I hope to see you in the hotel bar later. But first, I have one more announcement to make."

15

From Father to Son

Waiters circled the room with flutes of champagne. Once everyone had a glass, Cyril clinked his watch against his drink, and the murmur of conversations lowered to a soft din.

"Ladies and gentlemen, what a night! I want to thank all of you, from the bottom of my heart, for joining in on this auction. It was quite last minute and in an odd location, but it means the world to me that you were able to attend, especially since this will be the last Lost Masterpieces auction."

A wave of gasps rose up from the invitees.

"You'd said that you'd been working a lot of overtime lately, but I didn't realize you had gotten burned out," Gary said with true concern in his voice.

"Come now, Cyril, you just need a little time off and then you'll feel differently," Nico Manzino called out, his sentiment echoed by several guests.

"It would be such a shame for you to stop creating your masterful repeats," Countess Ursula agreed.

"It warms my heart to hear your words, but I have made up my mind. I want to retire later this year and am planning on handing my gallery over to my son, Cyprus. Which is why this is the last auction, and also why I felt it was important to allow more than one invitee to win all of the bids. Thank you for backing down, Serena."

He looked to Miss De Ville and bowed slightly. When she returned the gesture, she wore a tight smile on her face. I got the feeling that she now regretted giving in to his demand. His work would only increase in value, once his retirement was official.

"My son's vision is slightly different from my own. He won't be making copies as I have, but will soon share his own art with the world, instead. I'm proud of you, Cyprus, and can't wait to see what you do with the gallery."

When Cyril held up his glass, the young man in an old-fashioned tuxedo stepped forward and bowed.

"Gosh, he does look like Cyril, but too old to be his son," Rhonda whispered to me.

I'd noticed the resemblance earlier, too, but more compelling to me was how he had seemed completely uninterested in the paintings or guests. For that reason, I had discounted him as a potential player in the possible smuggling ring; if he planned to go in the same direction as his father, it would have behooved him to schmooze with all present, instead of keeping to himself all night.

"To Cyprus!"

I noticed that instead of toasting to Cyril's replacement, Manzino was fuming. Why was it so important that Cyril stay on as owner of Gallery Bouve? I would have to tell Myrtle about his odd behavior and odder conversation with Cyril that I'd overheard earlier this evening.

Cyril downed his drink, then smiled up at his invitees again. "Because the bidding process has taken significantly longer than I had anticipated—"

"No thanks to Serena," Johnny grumbled.

"Now, now, that's not necessary. It does mean that we will need to wrap this party up before the free port security escorts us out. Since we are all staying at the same hotel, I've arranged for a tab in the hotel bar, for those who wish to enjoy each other's company a little longer."

"That's generous of you," Gary said. "Seeing as this is your last go, I'll definitely have a drink on you."

It took a while to get everyone out of the free port and back into their rented limousines. When ours pulled up to the curb, I was thrilled to sink into the back seat and close my eyes during the short ride to our boutique hotel. Rhonda seemed to be even more tired than me and was softly snoring before our driver was through the free port's gates.

I hadn't quite dozed off when our limo slowed to a stop and our driver called out, "We've arrived."

Seconds later, the door opened. Rhonda stretched her arms above her head before thanking the young driver, who helped us both out. I usually refused a helping hand, but in this case, my heels kept getting caught up in the plush carpeting, making it difficult to get out of the limo, and I needed the leverage.

"Do you want to have a nightcap at the bar with the rest? I'd like to have one more drink, and then I think I'll be ready for bed," Rhonda said before covering her mouth to disguise a yawn.

I considered her words. As much as I wanted to listen in on the conversations at the bar, I had a more pressing matter to deal with. Dave seemed to believe that my boss had lent me to his organization, but I wanted to hear Reggie give me that order directly.

"If you don't mind, I'm going to take a shower first. I've got a killer headache—maybe the water will help."

"Oh, I have some aspirin in my purse. Would you like some?" my bestie said, her voice laced with concern. She was such a doll, I hated having to lie to her.

"That would be great, thanks." I gratefully took the pills I didn't actually need and held them in my palm. "I'll take them with a glass of water, once I get up to our room."

"That's smart. Why don't we head up? I'd like to touch up my makeup before coming back down, then the bathroom is all yours."

"Sounds good."

After Rhonda was finished, she left with a wave, leaving me alone. I turned the lock and called my boss.

"Hey, Carmen, thanks for calling me back so quickly. How is the assignment going so far?"

I had to suppress a laugh at his attempt to butter me up before telling me the real reason for his call. Reggie never concerned himself with the day-to-day operations, preferring to read his employees' summaries of the assignments after they were completed. He had company contacts, like Myrtle, to take care of the more pressing matters.

But I figured it was better to humor him by answering his question in a serious way—he was my boss, after all.

"Honestly, it's all a bit unclear right now. Cyril might be smuggling art, or it could be that he is trying to bamboozle his clients by selling multiple copies of the same repeat. Has Myrtle had a chance to check on the authenticity of the two confiscated paintings yet? I am beginning to think they are forgeries, as well. Cyril's work did fool many an expert over the years."

"That's part of what I wanted to talk with you about. Myrtle has already discussed the matter with the Italian police. They are one hundred percent certain that the paintings are genuine because two of their most trusted consultants verified their authenticity, independently of each other."

I frowned into the phone. "Well, that's another theory busted. Don't worry, I have a few more ideas to test. It could be that Cyril's not smuggling artwork, but that he's committing tax evasion. Or he might be whitewashing money for a criminal organization. Those theories are not my own, but ones I've been told about tonight."

Reggie was silent a moment. "So you have already had a chance to talk to Dave Swanson?"

"Oh, yes, in fact we had a nice long chat after we had both snuck into the gallery to examine Cyril's art."

"He didn't blow your cover, did he? I figured Dave would be too busy to fill you in right away."

My boss's concern and remark melted my irritation a smidgen. "I guess it was good timing that we both broke into the gallery when we did. During our few minutes alone, he did fill me in on his assignment and it does sound like we are on the same trail. But you could have warned me earlier that Dave was Interpol."

"I didn't know he was there, either, until his boss called me shortly before I messaged you. After he explained the urgency of the situation, he asked if I would temporarily lend you to Interpol so that you could work with Dave on this investigation. Trust me, if I'd had the opportunity, I would have talked with you about it first."

"It's good of you to say that." His words helped to further smooth my ruffled feathers.

"Dave's boss did mention that the operation may involve the Mafia," Reggie said. The hesitation in his voice told me that he was uncertain as to how I would react to the news.

My pulse quickened at the thought of finding a connection to the mob boss whom I suspected of murdering my husband. "With a little luck, it'll be Antonio Corozza's gang," I replied forcefully.

"Alright, so that news didn't scare you off. Remember that if you want to really hurt Corozza, you'd be better off trying to dismantle his network and forgetting about trying to get to him. However, there are a lot of criminal organizations active in Italy, and many are involved in large-scale robberies and smuggling. There's no guarantee that the mobster Dave is chasing is the same one you are."

"I do realize that," I huffed. "Speaking of mobsters, how are you coming along with decrypting Mac's phone?"

I had pickpocketed the phone of a gangster named Mac Mahoney during my last assignment, after learning that he was in contact with Corozza. I'd sent the password-protected device over to my boss, knowing Rosewood's team of computer geeks would have a better chance at breaking into his phone than I would. Corozza had gone underground soon after Carlos disappeared, leaving me chasing a ghost. I'd do just about anything to find a lead to his whereabouts.

"According to Myrtle, it's heavily encrypted, so it is going to take a while to decipher. Which means you would be better off forgetting about it for now and focusing on the task at hand. Dave's boss has ordered him to share any information he gathers with you, and I expect you to do the same."

It took me a moment to push my vengeful feelings about my husband's murderer aside before I could answer my boss in a normal tone. "After Dave told me that he was Interpol and explained the tax evasion angle, I shared the list of five paintings with him. He also told me that he's put trackers on all of the frames, so we can see where they go after they leave the free ports."

"Excellent, that's the spirit. Keep it up and I bet we'll finally break open this case. Who purchased the five paintings we are interested in?"

"A collector named Serena De Ville won four of the five bids and is having them shipped to Trieste for pickup. I sent her name to Myrtle earlier, so she could do a background check. Serena has a palazzo there and claims that she's been decorating it with Cyril's paintings, which justifies her choice of location."

"And the fifth?" Reggie's voice sounded oddly taut. It was only noticeable because he was usually so chill about everything. But when it came to catching Cyril Bouve, he had a strange edgy energy about him that didn't sit well with me.

"That is a portrait that was purchased by an American named Johnny Bighorn. He's picking it up from the Luxembourg free port tomorrow morning."

"What a relief," Reggie breathed.

"Excuse me?" I sucked in my breath.

"I'm relieved that one person did not win all of the bids. This gives us two chances to try to get a closer look at the art. Hopefully one or both of the buyers will be reasonable enough to allow us to examine them, once you and Dave can explain your suspicions to them. The Rosewood Agency may not be well-known among the general public, but Interpol is. It's a good thing you two are teaming up on this one."

His words were oddly rushed, but did make sense. I nodded slowly, even though Reggie could not see me. "I guess it is."

"I want you to follow Serena's four paintings to Italy."

I had to laugh. "She's probably the least reasonable of the two. Why don't I stick with the Bighorns? They are pretty easygoing, seem law-abiding, and get along well with Rhonda. I bet they'd have no problem with me taking a closer look at their painting, if I ask nicely."

"No, you have to go to Italy," Reggie stated rather brusquely. Why was my normally as-relaxed-as-a-Buddhist-monk boss getting so riled up by this case?

"There is only one of you, and if you can intercept Serena De Ville's shipment, you'll have four paintings to examine, not just one. I'll find another agent to deal with the Bighorns. With a little luck, they are going to fly straight home, and I can have a team examine it in Texas."

"True," I mumbled, but the niggling feeling that my boss was holding something back was only growing stronger. It wasn't like Reggie to hide things from his agents, and I only hoped that whatever it was wouldn't hinder my investigation.

But he was right; there was only one of me, and Dave and I were now a team. "Dave's already mentioned Trieste as a location of interest, I can imagine he'd also like to follow Serena's art to Italy. And it would be prudent to stick together until we figure out what exactly Cyril is up to."

"Excellent. Good luck in Italy, and keep Myrtle up to date, okay?" Reggie replied.

"Will do."

It was only after I'd hung up that I realized what was bothering me about our conversation. I hadn't mentioned to my boss that the Bighorns were from Texas.

16

So Many Possibilities

When I set off to find Dave and let him know that I'd talked to my boss, and that the two recovered portraits were genuine, he was still in his hotel room. As he opened the door, I noted that he'd changed out of his tuxedo and into a tailored suit that fit him like a glove. It took all of my willpower not to ogle him, but look him in the eye, as a professional should.

After I confirmed that we would team up for this investigation, his shoulders visibly relaxed, and he sank back into his hotel room's couch.

"So, what do you think Cyril's game plan is? Could Serena have bought the art for him, to ensure that it gets to Italy? It seems like a lot of trouble to go through for four paintings," I said as I plopped down next to him, figuring we might as well get to work.

"It is a way to keep his hands clean, and to ensure the transaction is official and recorded. But if she was supposed to buy all five, then our Texan friends messed up his plan."

"Yeah, I don't buy that Cyril accidentally overlooked their bid. I also thought it was strange that he refused to make their purchase official at the end of the party, so that the Bighorns could take the portrait to the hotel with them. It wouldn't have taken that long to complete the transaction," I said, before musing aloud, "Is it possible that Cyril is planning on stealing it from them?"

Dave sat straight up and locked eyes with me. "Or he might have his Mafia associates do it for him. Maybe we should alert the Texans or arrange for security. Their lives might be in danger."

"You make an excellent point. But for now, the artwork is inside the free port, which means both they and their portrait should be safe for the night."

Dave relaxed back into the couch. "Of course, you're right. It's been a long night. It's just so frustrating not knowing what we are really dealing with—tax evasion, whitewashing, or smuggling."

"I agree. But there isn't much more we can do tonight, except for look into chartering a jet to Trieste. That's where Serena is having her paintings shipped to. With a little luck, the charter service Rosewood prefers flies out of Luxembourg Airport."

He ran a hand through his dark brown hair. "Could I catch a ride? It would save me a lot of paperwork, and make it easier for us to stick together."

"Of course, my boss would insist upon it." A nagging thought popped to the surface of my thoughts. "But what about your partner, the one who'd fallen ill? Does she need a ride back, as well?"

"She's not my partner, but the niece of the lady whose invitation I used to get into the party. She took her aunt's jet back to Italy after she left the party, which is why I don't have a ride back down."

"That makes sense."

"And who are you traveling with—Rhonda Rhodes or Lady Sophie?"

I rolled my eyes before explaining what had happened since we'd last seen each other at the Moreaus' villa.

Dave had trouble keeping the grin off of his face. "Igor Thumpkin? That guy's won pretty much every kickboxing title that exists. You're both lucky that he's got a sweet spot for Lady Sophie, otherwise it could have ended much differently for you."

I looked away. "Yes, well, I'm glad Sophie's feeling better, but wish she'd stayed in the hospital. If her foot doesn't heal properly, I'll never be able to forgive myself."

Dave's eyebrows drew together. "Is this a girl thing? Lady Sophie knew you had someone qualified to take her place and that there was no need for her to come to the auction. Yet she did. Which means she chose to do this, and if her foot does not heal properly, it's not your fault. Right?"

"It must be a guy thing to be so callous. You're missing a lot of layers, but there is nothing I can do about it now. Although I am not letting her come to Trieste with us."

It wasn't just her foot that I was concerned about. I didn't want to have to explain why I was partnering with Dave for the rest of the assignment, at least not until we had already landed in Italy. Hearing that news now might make her think that she needed to tag along.

Dave stood up. "I was just about to head down to the bar. Would you care to join me?"

I rose, as well. "I want to check in with Lady Sophie first, but I'll come down after we've finished chatting."

"Sure, alright. See you there." He leaned in to kiss me on the cheek, but it just felt strange allowing another man to get so close, even after nearly four years of being alone. So I pulled back instinctively, then immediately regretted doing so. What was I afraid of—getting hurt again? Rhonda was right; there was nothing holding me back from starting over. Yet, Dave already had his hand on the door handle, and the mood was broken.

So I pushed my mixed emotions aside and set off for the Baroness's room. Unfortunately, her nurse refused me entrance, saying Lady Sophie was asleep and heavily medicated, but that she would mention that I had stopped by, once her ladyship woke back up.

So I headed downstairs, but by the time I got down to the bar, there was no one left except the three groups of investors, busy belting out karaoke tunes in the hotel's lounge. Dave and Rhonda were nowhere to be seen.

Not in the mood for a Beatles sing-along, I went back up to my hotel room to find Rhonda belting out show tunes as she showered. It was going to be a long night.

Too soon, my bestie was out of the shower and towel-drying her hair as she interrogated me. "Where were you? You didn't join in on the karaoke party, yet when I got back up here, the room was empty. So where did you go?"

"That's funny, I must have just missed you on the staircase. I'd taken a bath to let the aspirin take effect and I felt so good afterwards, I decided to join the party. But pretty much everyone was gone, so I came back up to the room. You were already in the shower when I got here," I said breezily, lying through my teeth like the professional I was.

"Wow, then the ventilation system in this room is amazing. There was no condensation whatsoever in the bathroom," Rhonda said. As the words left her mouth, I could see her brain putting the pieces together just before her lips formed that ridiculous O again. "Wait a second—were you in Dave's room? He came down to the bar for a minute or two, but left without even ordering a drink. Was he looking for you? Were you two messing around this whole time?"

I stared up at the ceiling. "No, I was not messing around with anyone. I did stop by Lady Sophie's room and chatted with her nurse for a minute before I went downstairs in the hope of running into you or Dave. But I swear, neither of you was there by the time I got to the lounge."

Rhonda pursed her lips as she studied my face, as if searching for a sign that I was lying. But after a few seconds of intense staring without result, she plopped down on the bed next to me.

"So what have you found out so far?"

After all of her slipups tonight, I didn't trust her to keep any intel to herself, so I relayed a heavily edited version of the evening's events.

"Nothing concrete so far, I'm afraid. Which is why my editor wants me to follow Serena's art to see where it gets delivered, after it leaves the free port in Trieste. I have a sneaking suspicion the delivery address will not be her palazzo."

Rhonda's eyes widened to saucers. "Does that mean you are going to Italy?"

"That is the plan." Now came the challenging part—how to convince Rhonda to stay here, instead of joining me. I needed to be able to respond quickly to any new lead Dave or I found while in Italy, and I didn't want Rhonda's presence to slow me down.

"You don't have to join me, you know. Why don't you fly out to Prague to be with Julie, and I'll meet you there once this is over?"

"Are you kidding me? You are going to Italy—of course I'm tagging along! Ralph and I were supposed to visit Rome and Florence during our honeymoon, but he got the stomach flu and we had to skip it. We can always visit Julie afterwards." I knew Rhonda missed her husband, Ralph, as much as I did Carlos, but she could talk freely about him and their lives together, without tearing up. I still wasn't at that point.

"Maybe you could fly down and meet me after I've completed my investigation. We don't know who all of the players are yet, and there are indications that the mob might be involved. I don't want to have to worry about your safety, as well as my own."

I could tell by her determined expression that Rhonda was having none of it. "Don't be ridiculous—I can take care of myself. Besides, I figure I can sightsee while you are gallivanting around Italy, tracking the stolen artwork. Trust me, I won't get in your way."

"True…" My voice faltered. Would it be so terrible if she tagged along? I would rather she not know that Dave was Interpol or that we were working together, but we'd already set the stage for a pretend relationship. I could just feed off of that until the assignment was complete. Reggie, however, might have a problem with her presence and wonder how much I had told her about the assignment. Rhonda was supposed to get me into the party, but nothing else.

I feigned a yawn and stretched my arms out over my head. "Golly, can we sleep on this? I am pooped. Let's talk about it in the morning, okay?"

"Sure thing," Rhonda replied in a cheery voice. But her scheming smile told me that she was not going to take "no" for an answer.

17

There Goes My Lead

Sirens woke me up the next morning.

"What's going on?" Rhonda asked groggily, her voice muffled by the thick duvet partially covering her face.

I was already up and at the window, a bedsheet wrapped around me like a toga. "I'm not sure, but the hotel's parking lot is full of cop cars."

Rhonda bolted straight up in bed. "But no fire trucks?"

"No. And the hotel would have alarms for that."

"That's a relief."

"Still, I want to see what's going on. Are you going to join me?"

Rhonda studied me as I pulled my pants on, both legs at once. "Yes, but not at such a frantic pace."

"Yeah, well, I guess it's part of being a journalist—you can't help but be inquisitive. I'll let you know what I find out."

I was fully dressed before Rhonda had gotten out of bed, and I rushed downstairs to see what the commotion was all about. It didn't take long to figure out. Policemen were swarming the lobby, and other officers were sitting with guests in the many wingback chairs filling the space, notebooks out and serious expressions on their faces.

"What's happened?" I asked a young officer, one of three currently blocking the main staircase.

"There has been an incident, and everyone in the hotel has to speak with a police officer before leaving the premises. Please wait here."

He turned his back to me and scanned the room, until a seated officer raised his arm, apparently signaling that he was free to interrogate someone.

The young one escorted me over to his older colleague. The interrogating officer seemed friendly enough, but quite tired. I was probably the umpteenth person he'd interviewed this morning, and it wasn't even seven o'clock yet. That set me at ease somewhat, hoping that he would be less alert and more prone to answering my questions, without realizing he was doing so.

With little pomp and no circumstance, he launched into his spiel. "There has been a murder, and I have to ask you a series of questions about your movements last night."

"A murder—was it Cyril Bouve?" A chill ran down my spine as I scanned the room, searching for the artist.

The officer pursed his lips as if he would rather not say, but immediately caved. Apparently I was not the first to have asked him that. "A man's body was found just outside the hotel's gate early this morning by a dog walker."

"Did he have any identification on his person?" I asked, immediately regretting how I had phrased the question.

As I feared, the officer cocked his head at me and seemed to study my face before finally replying, "No. Could I show you his photograph?" He began to turn over a picture clipped facedown to his clipboard, before adding, "It is rather graphic. If you would rather not…"

"No, it's fine. I don't mind a bit of blood," I replied, perhaps too eagerly. Nevertheless, the officer turned over the photo and handed it to me.

Darn, there goes my lead was my first thought. It was Enrico, the angry young man who had crashed Cyril's party last night. Maybe he was on to something, after all. And now neither I nor the police would be able to ask him about his assertions that Cyril was smuggling art and that Cyril's clients knew they were buying stolen paintings. How convenient.

He had been hit on the side of the head with something heavy, and the wound was gaping and gory. But the blood had congealed and turned a dark burgundy, meaning he had been dead for quite some time before this photo had been taken. Had he been killed last night, or early this morning? Either way, it could have been someone from this hotel who had lured him outside and bashed his head in. Or the killer may have run into him when they returned to the hotel after the auction last night and done him in.

Considering all of the rooms in this hotel were occupied by Cyril's guests, that pretty much meant I had wined and dined with a murderer last night.

"Madame, are you alright?" He pulled the photograph out of my fingers and turned it facedown again.

Had I been lost in thought for too long, or had my face paled as I considered what the framer's death meant to my investigation? Either way, my reaction had caused him visible concern.

"I'm fine, thanks. That is Enrico Greco; he came to Cyril Bouve's party last night, but he got into a verbal disagreement with a few of the guests and was escorted out fairly quickly."

"And what was the nature of these arguments?" The officer held a pen to his notepad. I wondered how much I should tell him. The last thing Interpol or the Rosewood Agency would want was for the local police to detain Cyril. So I lied a little, as I often had to do for my job, and softened the framer's accusations.

"It was hard to tell because Enrico was not making much sense. He started out by insulting several of the guests, until Cyril stepped in. Then he began ranting about how Cyril owed him money, but Cyril was quite adamant that that was not the case. In fact, he accused Enrico of stealing from him. Honestly, Enrico was ejected from the party before any of us knew what was happening."

As I was lying to the cop, I was adding "questioning the Texans" to my mental to-do list. Now that the framer was dead, they were my only way of finding out what that argument had been about. In theory, anyone could have killed Enrico—well, save the Baroness. Her wheelchair made it more challenging, if not impossible. But based on Enrico's threats last night, I really only suspected Cyril and the Texans at this stage.

Since I had little else to share about the guests or paintings, the officer was quickly finished with me. Yet instead of rushing back upstairs to update

Rhonda, I hung around the lobby to listen in. I sat down in a chair close to the dining room, as if I was waiting for someone, and pulled out my phone.

Quite soon my patience was rewarded when Cyril arrived downstairs and was called over to speak to the officer seated behind me. That interview quickly turned into a eulogy.

"He was like a son to me. If Enrico had not stolen supplies from me, I never would have fired him. His poor parents; they are going to be heartbroken."

His words became increasingly difficult to follow, until at one point, he seemed to be bawling. Which was why I tuned him out and focused my ears on Nico Manzino, being interviewed a few chairs to my left. With a slight turn of my head I could see him, without actually having to make eye contact.

At least Cyril seemed to have been affected by Enrico's death. Manzino, on the other hand, didn't seem to care at all about the murder, but was more put out that the investigation was delaying his flight home. During the short interview, he shared nothing new, until the officer began questioning Nico about his account of his own movements last night.

"I didn't see Enrico again, not after he was kicked out of the auction. I don't care what you think you saw on your security camera footage."

"Sir, are you denying that you came down to the lobby just after midnight last night?"

Manzino began to do just that, before pausing and shaking his head. "Wait a moment—how embarrassing. I did go down to the lobby, to ask for an aspirin. I drank too much at the auction and had a splitting headache."

"And did you speak with Enrico at that time? He was also seen in the lobby area around midnight. Unfortunately the hotel's cameras are only directed on the reception desk, not the rest of the spaces."

"No, I did not see him again. I took the aspirin upstairs and then went to bed."

I pondered his words. Had he used the same fib that I had with Rhonda, or had he really had a headache last night?

The officer dutifully wrote down the Italian's words before snapping his notebook shut. "Okay. Thank you for your time."

"Am I free to fly back to Italy?"

"Yes, we have your passport number and contact information. We will be in touch if we need to ask any more questions. Which means you are free to go."

The officer's words brought joy to Manzino's face. I had a sneaking suspicion that I needed to add the Italian to my suspect list, as well.

18

Shipping Snafu

After both art dealers were finished with the police, I headed upstairs, to update Rhonda. Yet when I saw the Baroness roll out of the lobby elevator, I changed direction.

"Lady Sophie, how you are doing today?" I always used her title properly in public, though I refused to curtsy.

Her nurse must have helped her with her makeup and hair, I figured, because both were way off the mark. She'd gone heavy with the rouge and eyeshadow, making Sophie appear to be far older than her sixty years, and her bob was not as neat as I was used to seeing it. Nevertheless, the Baroness was dressed impeccably in a silver ballgown accented with a sapphire necklace. The cut of the gems matched that of the diamonds in her tiara.

"I've had better nights," she said, keeping her tone and expression stoic.

Her nurse scoffed at Sophie's remark. "She was up for most of it. It can't be comfortable sleeping with your foot in a sling."

"Enough!" Sophie growled, causing her nurse's mouth to snap closed.

"The pain medication doesn't seem to be as effective here as it was in the hospital, that's all. It was difficult to drift off," she added in a gentler tone.

"It can't help that you are moving around so much," I added, not wanting to show too much sympathy, seeing as I was about to tell her to stay put. "Hey listen, Reggie wants me to follow Serena's art to Italy, but I am forbidding you from coming. You have to think of your health. Frankly, I don't want

Rhonda to come, either."

"You shouldn't need her, that's true," Sophie said, before pausing to ponder my words. "As much as I would like to fly down with you, I fear it would be too much for me right now. However, I do intend to attend the next party on our itinerary. It's being hosted by a good friend, and fractured foot or not, I am going to that one!"

"Let's see how you feel in a few days, alright? I'm just glad you are willing to sit this one out, no pun intended."

A glimmer of a smile crossed her face. I could imagine it was relief that she couldn't follow along on the next part of our journey, but had to stay behind and rest.

"Would you care to join me for breakfast?"

The Baroness looked to the lobby, still full of police officers. "I would rather get this police interview over with. Afterwards, I'll have a light meal, but I'd prefer to have it in my room."

"Fair enough." I patted her arm, then continued on my journey. Yet, before I could mount the first step, Rhonda's laugh drew me to the dining hall. Sure enough, my bestie was already seated and had a full plate in front of her.

"How the heck did you get around the cops? Weren't you supposed to be interviewed before you had breakfast?"

"I told that young one that if I didn't get sugar into my body first, I would have a diabetic meltdown."

I cocked my head at her. "But you aren't diabetic."

"He doesn't know that." Rhonda replied with a wink. "Grab a plate and join me."

I glanced around the room and noted that almost all of the guests were present. Cyril, Manzino, Countess Ursula, and Serena had yet to join us, however.

The artist soon entered, and he kept his head bowed as if he had something important on his mind. That didn't stop the Texans from cornering him.

"Cops or no cops, we have some unfinished business that I am itching to conclude," Johnny said.

"Thanks for not saying 'dying,' Johnny. It's already been such a strange morning," his wife added.

"Indeed, it has. So Cyril, what do you say we skip breakfast and head on over to the free port and get me my painting?"

Cyril pressed his fingertips against his temple. "I have more bad news. Your painting is no longer in Luxembourg, but is on its way to Italy."

Johnny jerked back, as if he'd been bitten by a snake. "What did you just say?"

"There was a terrible mix-up with the order slip. Somehow Serena was still listed as the winner of the bid, and your painting was crated up with her four. It is already in a truck on its way to Italy."

"Well, tell them to pull over and send another one down to pick mine up!"

"If only it were that simple. The paintings are in a secured truck that can't be opened until it reaches Trieste. I'll have your portrait sent to your home, free of charge."

"But we wanted to take advantage of the lower tax rate in Luxembourg. It's seventeen percent here, not twenty-two percent like in Italy," Josie explained. Which was a good thing, considering her husband was so red in the face, I was seriously wondering whether we would have to soon call an ambulance.

Cyril wrung his hands together. "I'm happy to pay the taxes; please don't worry about that. Your portrait will be on its way to Texas in no time."

"It's not the money; I want my painting!" Johnny bellowed. Practically everyone in the dining room seemed to stop and stare at the grown man, throwing a hissy fit like only a millionaire could.

Wow, what a baby, I thought. They seemed so down to earth, but then again, you only see what people want you to see. And stressful situations usually brought out the true character of a person.

Johnny pushed up the brim of his hat, his nostrils flaring. "Wait a second— are you sure it was a mix-up? Serena's always trying to one-up me, and she was trying pretty hard to get her hands on that portrait."

"Serena had nothing to do with this! It was a silly mistake made by the free port's transportation department, that is all," Cyril cried.

"Well, I'm not leaving Europe without my painting."

By the steadfastness of Johnny's tone, I'd say that Cyril had a real problem.

"I'm telling you the truth—I cannot stop the shipment even if I wanted to. However, I can have it returned to Luxembourg immediately. It would be back within two days."

Johnny looked to his wife, who shook her head. "Nope, that's not good enough. We aren't staying in Luxembourg for another two days. I guess we have no choice but to fly to Italy."

"Excuse me?" Cyril's squealed response was girlishly high-pitched. But why would he care? Unless he was hoping to have the painting to himself, at least long enough to do whatever nefarious activity he was planning on committing. The painting's accidental trip to Italy did help support my smuggling theory, Dave's whitewashing theory, and our joint theory on potential ties to the Mafia. Dave would have to get ahold of the customs form and see how much Cyril had valued it for, once it left Trieste.

"You do not have to fly to—" Cyril began in a shrill voice, but Johnny held up a hand to silence him.

"My mind is made up. I'm picking my portrait up from the free port in Trieste. Anyone fancy a trip to Venice?"

19

A Flight To Venice

"That's really not necessary!" Cyril protested again.

"Venice? I thought you were heading to Trieste," Rhonda said.

"Venice is just on the other side of the bay. We'll stay in the city tonight and take a taxi over to the free port in the morning," Josie explained.

Johnny half bowed to my bestie. "If you don't have any other pressing plans, why not join us for a few days?"

"Visiting Venice would be a dream come true!" Rhonda clapped her hands together before turning to me. "What a coincidence that you had me bid on Canaletto's *View of the Grand Canal* during the auction. It must be a sign from above! We have to go—don't you think, Carmen?"

I tried to catch my friend's eye, but hers were already glazing over as her head filled with visions of Italy, I suspected. Why did Rhonda have to blurt that out? Surely the Bighorns would find it strange that I was asking my friend to bid on paintings. And yet, they didn't seem to notice her remark. They were either incredibly incurious people or just hard of hearing.

"Then it's settled—you have to come. There is plenty of room in our private jet," Josie declared.

Rhonda fiddled with the hem of her jacket, as if she was still uncertain she was welcome, despite their reassurances. "Are you sure?"

"Of course; the more people to split the jet fuel costs with, the better," Johnny said, barely hiding a smile.

Rhonda's mouth gaped open until the Texans burst out laughing. "Oh, the look on your face!"

Rhonda joined in. "I get it—rich people humor."

"Seriously, the more the merrier. Carmen, would you like to join us, too?"

When Josie turned to me, I put on my happy face and cried out, "That would be great!"

And I meant it. It would have been much easier to fly down without Rhonda by my side. Yet, if she was going to be in Venice anyway, it would be better for us to join the Bighorns now, than to try to meet up with them in Italy. All I had to do was ensure that we planned a couple of sightseeing adventures together on the ride down, so that Rhonda would stay occupied. I could always feign a stomach cramp and bow out at the last minute, so that Dave and I could follow up on any new leads.

Rhonda's expression grew pensive. "You know, I just had a crazy idea. I always wanted to visit Italy with my Ralph, but it never happened. Samantha, that's my youngest one, she wouldn't be interested enough to even apply for a passport. But Julie is here in Europe. Instead of us going to Prague, why don't I invite her to join us in Venice, Carmen? Wouldn't that be a kick to see part of Italy with her, instead?"

I could tell Rhonda's new "I just faced death and survived" attitude was still influencing her decisions; she would never have dared to open herself up to such bitter disappointment otherwise. The chance of her eldest dropping everything to join her in Venice for the weekend was pretty much null.

"Who's Julie?" Josie asked.

"My oldest daughter. She's working in Prague at the American Embassy. I'm so proud of her adventurous spirit, as was her father."

"That would be wonderful if your daughter could join us! You should call her right now," Josie cried.

This conversation felt like a freight train racing off of a cliff, and there was nothing I could do to stop it. "Wouldn't it be more relaxed to fly to Prague, after everything's been sorted with the Bighorns' painting? Julie probably couldn't get away from work, anyway."

Yet my words fell on deaf ears. Rhonda and Josie were already hugging.

After they pulled apart, Rhonda said to Josie in a gentle voice, "I'm going to call my daughter right now."

Then she turned to glare at me. "What's wrong with you? You're acting like you don't want Julie to join us."

"No, it's not that! I bet she has to work, that's all."

I wasn't trying to be cruel by dissuading her from calling her daughter; in fact, I was trying to be a good friend. Julie hadn't made time for her mom in years. Rhonda couldn't expect her to suddenly change or act differently, and I hated to see my friend get hurt.

"Well, it's Friday, and the Embassy can't require her to work seven days a week, can they? I bet she could get away for the weekend, if she wants to."

Therein lies the problem, I thought. Would Julie want to? Based on her behavior these past few years, my answer would be no. But I couldn't say that to Rhonda, especially not in front of the Bighorns. It was not only embarrassing, but perhaps condescending. Besides, I didn't have kids and didn't know enough about the complexities of those parent-child relationships to provide any sage advice.

"No, you're right. We can always go to Prague and spend more time with her, later, if she can't join us in Venice," I added, hoping to temper my bestie's expectations.

"That's exactly what I'm thinking. See you in a minute," Rhonda called out, already halfway to the dining room's entrance and on her way up to our room, I suspected.

As I watched her walk away, I silently prayed that her conversation would not leave her in tears. In case it did, I decided to follow her up, figuring I could always stand in the hallway until I heard her wailing. At least I could be there for her, even if Julie was not.

I pushed my chair back, just as Dave spoke up, scaring the bejesus out of me. Some agent I was—I hadn't even noticed him standing behind us, presumably listening in on our conversation.

"Would it be audacious of me to ask if I could tag along?" he asked. "My companion took the jet back to Italy already, and I do have to return to Venice to meet with a client."

I about slapped my forehead, forgetting that I had offered him a ride earlier. Luckily, Josie didn't seem bothered by his assertiveness.

"Golly, of course you can hitch a ride," she said.

Relieved that the situation with Dave had been so easily resolved, I stood to go and find Rhonda. Yet before I could get out of my chair, I noticed Gary bearing down fast, his sights set on last night's auctioneer. "Hey, where's my artwork, Cyril? Is it on its way to Italy, too?" His worried expression was in sharp contrast with his smug tone.

"No, it is still in Luxembourg. Everything has been arranged with customs, and your painting will be delivered to the hotel this afternoon."

"How convenient for Gary that his art wasn't whisked off to Trieste," Johnny pouted.

"What did you say, old boy?" Cyril said, but Serena's entrance interrupted their spat and drowned out Johnny's snide answer. I could imagine it was as much her magnetic presence as the fuchsia pantsuit that she had donned that drew their attention.

The former model leaned her lanky body against the doorframe, tilted up her chin, and laid the back of her palm against her forehead. "The police are acting as if we are the criminals!"

"I agree completely," Cyril added as he rushed over to her, and away from the Texans. "I don't know why they think one of my guests killed him."

"Probably because he was murdered in front of a hotel that is filled with your guests, and only your guests?" I couldn't help myself—Cyril's woe-is-me routine was grating on my nerves.

But he and Serena ignored me. "I'm quite put out by the whole ordeal. As soon as Bobby's done talking to the police, I'm jetting off to Paris for some shopping therapy," the former model said.

I knew she meant it literally, and wondered how much she would have to spend before she felt better.

"You'll have my art delivered to my palazzo, per usual, won't you, Cyril? My housekeeper is always home."

"Of course." Cyril lunged forward in an attempt to kiss her hand, but Serena was too busy with herself to notice. As she wafted out of the dining area and presumably back up to her room, the Baroness and her nurse rolled in.

Cyril turned his charms on to my partner. "Lady Sophie, it is good of you to join us."

"Certainly, though it will not be for long. I agree with Serena; the police interviews were most exhausting. However, I won't be engaging in any shopping therapy anytime soon." She looked to her foot, raised up in front of her.

"You poor thing," Cyril murmured.

"Would you like to join us in Venice? We're all going down to pick up my painting that Cyril here had sent to Trieste," Johnny explained.

"I assure you, it was a mistake, and I am doing all I can to rectify the situation. As far as Baroness Rutherford is concerned, she can fly down with me. I have plenty of room in my jet for you and your nurse, your ladyship," Cyril added.

Sophie only raised a well-manicured eyebrow. "Gentlemen, I thank you both for your offer, but I fear that Venice is not an easy place to get around whilst confined to a wheelchair. I would prefer to stay here and rest. However, before you leave, I would love to have brunch with you, Cyril, if you have no other engagements?"

"For you, I will make the time."

"Excellent."

After the Baroness nodded her head slightly in Cyril's direction, he turned to the rest of us. "I have some business to conduct before flying down to Venice, but should be there before your portrait arrives in Trieste later this evening. I will be staying at the Residenza Venezia and highly recommend it. As soon as I know more about your painting's whereabouts, I will contact you. Now, if you will excuse me, I have a date with this lovely lady."

He smiled down at the Baroness, who did her best to flutter her eyelashes, but her nurse had applied so much mascara, they clumped together, instead.

However, when Cyril turned to follow her to a table, he caught sight of something in the lobby that made him freeze.

"Cyril?" Sophie asked, seeming to notice that he was no longer following.

"I need to talk to Manzino for a moment about this mix-up. I won't be a minute, then I'll join you. Is that alright?"

"Certainly."

When the Baroness's nurse pushed her over to a vacant table, Johnny turned to the rest of us and slapped his hands together. "Okay folks, why don't we meet downstairs in two hours? That should give us enough time to pack, and my crew a chance to ready the jet."

"Sure thing." I couldn't help but giggle. Thanks to my assignments, I was used to living the high life, and private jets were definitely a part of that lifestyle. But Rhonda, despite her enormous wealth, rarely indulged in the finer things in life. I couldn't wait to see how she reacted during our flight down.

20

Leaving on a Jet Plane

When I got back to the hotel room, Rhonda threw her arms around my neck as soon as I entered.

"Julie can fly down for the weekend. She's going to meet us in Venice tonight. Isn't that amazing?"

I bent my head down so I could push up my jaw before she saw that it had flapped open, then gave my friend a big hug, wondering why Julie had said yes. "Yes, amazing indeed. I'm so glad for you."

Something didn't make sense. After all of these years of ignoring her mother, now she was going to drop everything to spend the weekend with her?

Even worse, I knew this news would definitely upset the Baroness. Having Rhonda's daughter tag along was quite amateurish. But did I need to tell my partner? There was no real reason for her to know about Julie's presence in Venice. And having her there would help keep Rhonda occupied and out of my hair, especially if the Bighorns preferred to do something romantic as a couple.

"Say, we better get packed up. Johnny and Josie want us to meet them in the lobby in just under two hours."

"That's plenty of time, especially if I hustle." Rhonda grabbed her suitcase and started shoveling her clothes inside. "Is it warmer in Italy than here? What kinds of clothes should we take with us?"

I stared at my own open suitcase, wondering what to pack, when it hit me. "I suppose we had better pack everything with us. There's no reason to come back to Luxembourg, so we might as well check out. We can book our next flight from Venice."

Rhonda whipped her head over, a wide grin on her face. "We can, can't we? This is so exciting, and it feels like a real adventure, just like I was hoping to have! Jetting around Europe with my best friend—it's a pretty good life."

I grinned over at her. "Yes, it is."

Yet her words reminded me that she was only here jetting around Europe, because Sophie could not. And my partner, who had been pretty rude to her earlier, had not yet apologized. It would be nice if they could talk things out before we flew off to Italy, so that there would be no hard feelings later, on either side.

"Say, Rhonda, could we take a quick break and pop back down to the lobby? Lady Sophie requested your presence before we left," I lied, "but I wasn't certain if we would have time to visit, given that we had to pack up. But it looks like you're almost done and we still have an hour and a half before departure."

The way she glared at me, I could tell that she wanted to see her ladyship before we left. I just hoped Sophie would understand why I was making her chat with my friend, and that she'd do the right thing and say she was sorry.

"Why didn't you say so earlier? Of course I'll make time for Lady Sophie. Is she down in the dining hall?"

"Yep, at least she was a few minutes ago."

"Well, what are we waiting for? Let's get down there." Rhonda practically ran down the short flight of stairs to the lobby, and then beelined over to the dining area in search of my partner. I had to jog to keep up. Rhonda sure did seem fascinated with Sophie, or at least her royal background and title.

I only hoped that Cyril was still occupied with Manzino, and not sitting down to brunch with the Baroness. I picked up my pace to catch up to Rhonda, wanting to ensure she didn't accidentally butt in on their meal and say something compromising or embarrassing.

Luckily for me, Cyril was still engaged in a gesture-filled conversation with Manzino at the back of the lobby. There was no way I could get close enough to hear what they were saying without them noticing, so I let it go and instead focused on my original goal of getting Sophie to apologize to Rhonda.

I hadn't briefed my partner on my reason for coming back down, but she seemed to pick up on the hint as soon as Rhonda crossed over to her.

"Lady Sophie, I heard from Carmen that you aren't going to be joining us in Italy. I do hope you feel better, and aren't too upset with me still. I don't know what it is about Cyril, but that man gives me the jitters." Rhonda kept her eyes averted as she spoke, as if she was afraid of offending Sophie with her gaze.

Thankfully my partner knew what she had to do to make things right between us. She grabbed my friend's hand and squeezed it tight. "Dear Rhonda, I do apologize for my snobbish behavior during the party. Cyril is quite snooty himself, and I needed him to trust me. I did not mean any of the horrid things that I said last night. Please forgive me if I embarrassed you, but I do hope because of that performance, he will open up to me about his role in this operation, once the rest of you have left."

I could see Rhonda's posture straightening with every word. "Hon, I understand completely. You were playing a part, and you did it marvelously. I sure do hope you find the answers we're all looking for. Good luck."

Before I could stop her, Rhonda bear-hugged my partner, leaving Sophie speechless. It seemed like hours before she released my partner from her grip and stepped back.

I leaned over to Sophie's ear. "Thank you, and good luck with Cyril. I'll call once we're in Italy."

"Excellent, now please get your charming friend out of here. It looks like Cyril and Manzino are wrapping things up, and him running into her now might ruin everything."

"Of course, we'll talk later."

When I saw Cyril stride away from Manzino, I gently pushed on Rhonda's back, moving her out of the dining room as fast as our heels would allow.

Once we got back up to the room, finishing packing was a breeze. I figured we were early, yet when we took the elevator down to the lobby, Dave, Josie, and Johnny were waiting for us.

"Oh, gosh, are we late?" I looked at my watch.

"Not at all! We were on the elevator just before you. If everyone is ready, let's skedaddle!" Johnny said.

A short taxi ride later, and we were boarding the Bighorns' private jet, a spacious Gulfstream G280 worth about thirty million dollars. Johnny wasn't lying; there was plenty of room for us all, and several more passengers.

Once we'd taken off and were flying at altitude, Johnny knocked on one of the windows. "It's a great view, isn't it? Private jets fly lower than commercial airliners, so we can see more of the landscape."

"It is," I confirmed, also intrigued by the closeness of the winding rivers and patchwork of fields we were flying over.

"So that's why we can see so much! It's wonderful," Rhonda enthused.

"Your jet must be even bigger than ours, if you are used to flying at higher altitudes. Which model do you have?" Johnny asked.

Rhonda guffawed. "I don't own a private jet! First class on a commercial line is already a luxury, as far as I'm concerned."

"Aren't you sweet!" Josie exclaimed, and for a moment, I thought she was going to pinch my friend's cheeks. Had Josie or Johnny ever ridden on a commercial airline? I somehow doubted it.

"You should consider buying one, or joining one of those timeshares. That's how we started out. Once you get access to one, you'll think up plenty of places to go."

"That may be, but I don't see myself getting one in the near future." Rhonda added, a touch more shyly. My bestie was ridiculously wealthy, but didn't like to show it. She still drove her old Volvo with a ding in one side, and lived in the same neighborhood she had grown up in, admittedly in a much larger house. Her one vice was clothes—and plenty of them. I rarely saw her wear the same outfit twice, even on our vacation so far.

"I must apologize in advance, but we don't bother with a stewardess when we're over in Europe. The flights are all so short that it's not really necessary to have someone onboard to cook our food or serve us drinks. But the bar is open, and my Johnny is quite the cocktail mixer. Just let us know what you'd like. I'm going to start with a glass of chilled Dom Perignon." Josie stepped behind the bar and grabbed a bottle out of the mini-refrigerator.

"That sounds heavenly," Rhonda gushed.

"I would love a glass of bubbly, if you're offering," I added.

"Could I have a shot of bourbon neat?" Dave asked.

Johnny sprung up, as if he was glad to be of service, too. "You bet, coming right up." From a cabinet, he pulled out a bottle and two shot glasses, filling each to the brim. "*Salute.*"

"Cheers."

Once we'd all been served and had swiveled our plush leather seats so we were facing each other, Josie leaned forward and toyed with the champagne glass in her hand. "So, Dave, who is this client of yours and why did your companion abandon you in Luxembourg?"

"Oh, she didn't abandon me," he said with a laugh. "She had stomach trouble and wanted to fly back to Italy last night, instead of toughing it out in the hotel."

"That's too bad; from what Manzino said, she is quite lovely. Are you two dating?"

Dave blushed at the remark. "Nico did have an eye on her. No, she's not my girlfriend, but the niece of my client, Dottoressa Bianci, an elderly art lover who had taken ill a few days before the auction. Which is why she gave her ticket to her niece and asked me to accompany her, to bid in her place. I've been helping the Dottoressa get her collection in order, and have access to all of her financial accounts. Her niece is a lovely woman, but doesn't know much about artwork or her aunt's tastes, and it was my task to enlighten her."

"Still, it was quite nasty of her to leave you in a lurch like that. Why did you stay at the auction, instead of flying back with her?" Josie asked.

Dave shrugged. "I had to stay so I could bid on the paintings I thought the Dottoressa would enjoy. I only won one bid and it cost more than I'd hoped, but it will please her immensely, so it was worth it. Especially now that Cyril is retiring—it makes his work worth even more."

"That's a great point! I didn't even think of how his retirement would affect the price. I'm pretty pleased with our purchase, as well. I just wish Cyril hadn't mixed up the delivery," Johnny moped.

"Well, if he hadn't, we wouldn't be flying off to Italy for a few days, would we? So I guess we should all thank Cyril for messing up," Josie laughed, clearly done with Johnny's ploys for sympathy.

"Say, it sounds like you know Cyril pretty well. How often have you attended these lost art auctions?" I asked, figuring now was as good a time as any to subtly interrogate the Bighorns.

"We've been to three of them. Cyril tends to invite the same core group of guests, and a few other new invitees to help keep the bidding high. We can't always make it over, but we do try. I enjoy seeing what he's been working on during the previous year."

Dave made a point of staring into his drink, apparently happy to let me handle this part of the interrogation alone.

"Is that where you had met that framer, Enrico—at a previous auction?"

Josie's friendly demeanor shifted, and her eyes narrowed. "I don't know what that young man was thinking, but we don't buy stolen art! I love Cyril's idea of bringing back lost masterpieces, but they are copies, not the real thing. Heck, we only paid one hundred and fifty thousand for that portrait. If it is a real Manet, we sure did get it for a steal!"

Johnny nodded along. "That boy was crazy. He must have been trying to extort money out of Cyril by embarrassing him with those lies."

I side-eyed the Texans, wondering what their real backstory was. As much as I wanted to believe they were nothing more than art lovers falsely accused by the framer, it was odd how they had been singled out at the auction. And now they were being so tenacious about getting their hands on this painting—what Josie admitted was nothing more than a replica of a lost masterpiece.

On the other hand, it was not unusual for the absurdly rich to expect instant gratification, and that they would get their way at all times. And Cyril had messed up their delivery, in a way that almost seemed intentional—as if he didn't want the Texans to have it. If I was them, I would also be suspicious that Cyril or Serena had a hand in the mix-up.

Yet something about their willingness to fly down to Venice to retrieve their painting, instead of allowing Cyril to fly it back up to Luxembourg, or even send it directly to their home in Texas, didn't sit right with me. Whatever their reason, they were definitely worth checking out. I'd have to ask Myrtle to prioritize their background checks as soon as I had a moment alone.

I considered asking Rhonda what she thought of them, but knew that she wouldn't be able to keep my interest to herself, especially in light of the bond she and the couple had formed. So I kept my lips zipped and eyes opened, hoping their relaxed conversation with my bestie would reveal something useful.

After it was apparent they were going to chat about everything except for Cyril or his art, I figured I wasn't going to learn much more from the Texans anytime soon. So I tuned the others out and closed my eyes, letting myself half doze for the remainder of our short flight.

It was easy to do in the comfortable leather chairs, at least until I heard Rhonda say, "We are best friends, that's not a lie. But like I was telling Julie last night, she's the reason why we attended that auction. Carmen is really an undercover journalist writing a story about art smugglers, and she thinks Cyril or someone at the auction may be involved. Isn't that exciting? I bet that's why she asked you about that framer, Enrico."

My eyes shot open. "Hey, that was supposed to be a secret." Boy, was I glad that I hadn't shared my suspicions about the Bighorns with her.

"But the party is over. So what does it matter now?" Rhonda asked.

Dave seemed to be as confused as I was, probably because my bestie had shared another version of reality than I had with him.

The Texans were unusually quiet, seeming more interested in their airplane's carpeting than in me. Which I found to be an exceedingly strange reaction. If I had learned such a thing about my fellow passenger, I would be asking them a million questions. I'd already had my concerns about them, but my suspicions increased manyfold, thanks to their reaction.

"So, what did you find out?" Rhonda asked, oblivious to the change in my mood or my seething expression.

Why is she making me walk this delicate tightrope? "Not much, at least not that I can share right now. It is meant to be an investigative report, remember? My editor wouldn't appreciate me sharing my findings pre-publication."

"Oh, shoot, I didn't think it mattered. But from the way you're glaring at me, you obviously didn't want me telling anyone. I'm sorry, Carmen."

Johnny looked to his watch. "Well, I'll be. We should be starting our descent any minute. I'm going to check in with our pilot."

"I'll clean up our drinks. Better to do it now than when we're already descending." Josie sprung up and set about clearing the dishes from the small tables.

"Let me help," Rhonda said as she jumped up.

"Golly, you don't have to, but I won't say no."

21

Family Reunion

After our short flight, we stepped into the arrival hall at Venice's Marco Polo Airport, and the first thing I saw was Julie in the distance, searching the new arrivals for a familiar face.

I let out a cry of joy, glad to see my goddaughter in the flesh again, waving my hand over my head as I did. "Julie—over here!"

"Aunt Carmen!" she squealed and rushed towards my voice. Her words were a lie, but still music to my ears. We weren't blood relatives, but I'd known her since her birth, and during her baptism I had been officially deemed her "god-aunt." "Godmother" had too much of a Mafia ring for my taste.

In all honesty, I wasn't much of an aunt, but then Julie didn't want to be treated like a kid or mothered, so it all worked out.

"Is my baby here already?" Rhonda's voice rose an octave. She had been convinced Julie would meet us at the hotel later tonight, not at the airport. Yet here she was. Before Rhonda could even set her sights on her daughter, her cheeks were glistening with tears.

Julie, luckily a head taller than her mom and thus easier to spot, snaked her way through the crowd. As soon as she was in front of us, Rhonda let out a shriek that I was certain would bring security racing over. "Julie!"

Before the young woman could react, Rhonda had her wrapped up in a bear hug, and was swinging her to and fro so vigorously, I was worried she might just break Julie's back. "Oh, my baby girl! I thought I would never see you again!"

Julie's expression grew increasingly confused with Rhonda's every word. "What are you talking about? It hasn't been that long since we spoke. You didn't seriously think I was going to ignore you forever, did you?"

It took me a moment to realize that Rhonda was probably referring to our recent brush with death. An event Julie had not yet heard about, as far as I knew. During what we feared would be our last heart-to-heart, Rhonda had confessed that she deeply regretted losing contact with her oldest daughter.

Julie's sarcastic reply seemed to hit Rhonda harder than I could have anticipated. A torrent of emotion rushed through her body, causing her to alternatively wail, then hug Julie so tight, the girl looked to be short on breath.

I stood back, unsure what to do. I'd never seen my friend so distraught before.

"I'm so sorry, I just can't get my emotions under control," Rhonda sniffled, while hanging onto Julie as if she was a life buoy.

"Darling, why don't we splash some water on your face?" Josie said, her voice tinged with concern. She had been standing quietly by while mother and daughter reunited, but I was glad she chose now to intervene. As much as I wanted to help my friend, I knew I could better do so in another way—one that Josie could not.

"Thanks, Josie, I really appreciate it," I said, helping her to peel Rhonda's arms off of her daughter's bicep. When Josie led her off to the restrooms, I pulled Julie in the other direction, not wanting the rest to hear our conversation.

"Hey, how's my goddaughter?" Luckily, Jules and I always got along well. Perhaps because we both had a wide range of interests, a sarcastic sense of humor, and a taste for travel. Rhonda was right; we did have quite a bit in common.

I had always nurtured the impression that she could tell me anything—even things that she wouldn't dare discuss with her own mother. Which was why I figured she would tell me why she'd been avoiding Rhonda since

Ralph died.

"I *was* fine. What was that all about?"

Julie's irritated tone grated on my nerves. Partially because I had assumed she knew why Rhonda was so upset. "Your mom's emotional dam just burst."

She looked over at me blankly.

"Sorry to jump right in with this, but Rhonda's going to be back any minute. Did your mom do something to upset you? She sure thinks she did. And is that why you have been ignoring her for the past few months?"

Julie chewed on her lip. "Has it been so long since we spoke?"

"That's what Rhonda said. And she said that since your dad died, you haven't been back home. So what did she do?"

"Mom didn't do anything. I guess I've been so focused on getting a grip on my new job, I forgot to check in with the home front. Sam was always there for Mom, so I figured she was in good hands. Maybe I shouldn't have done that. It's not that she hasn't been on my mind; I just didn't think about calling."

I leaned back on my heel, my anger subsiding with her answer. "Alright, that makes sense. What are you doing these days? You mom thinks you are working at an embassy in Prague. She said you were up to your eyeballs in visa renewal paperwork—and had to work most weekends to keep up. But I've never heard of embassy personnel working as much overtime as she thinks you do. So, what's the real story?"

Julie glanced at the bathroom door, still closed, before lowering her voice. "I did start out at the embassy, but I didn't earn a master's degree in international relations to assist drunken tourists and renew passports. It was so boring and not what I hoped for."

When she stared off in the distance again, seemingly contemplating whether to continue or not, I took her hand, causing her to make eye contact, hoping our bond was still strong enough for her to trust me.

"You can tell me anything, without having to fear that I'll blab it straight to your mother."

That seemed to reassure her enough that she felt comfortable confiding in me. "Good, because I haven't told Mom yet, but another organization reached out to me recently and I liked what they had to offer. I'm enjoying my new position, but it's taking longer to get into the groove than I had expected. I figured once I'd gotten a better handle on it, I would tell her all about it. Honestly, so much has happened recently, it felt like it had only been a few weeks since we talked, not months."

I tried to recall how it was to be in my late twenties and early thirties, excited about my new career and devoting every waking moment to making myself the best in my field. I can imagine I ignored my mother quite a bit back then and didn't even notice. "That's amazing. Who do you work for now?"

But Julie didn't seem to have heard me. "It probably doesn't help that Sam lives in the same city as Mom and they see each other all the time. Sam said she even took care of her kids during their school's summer break. If Mom expects me to be around as much as my sister is, then she is going to be sorely mistaken. I'm not ready to settle down."

I knew better than to take sides between Sam or Julie, knowing that as much as the girls were friendly with each other, there had been an underlying competition present between them since birth, one I supposed was an integral part of being a sibling.

"It's good to know that you two have stayed in touch," I said as diplomatically as possible, wondering whether Rhonda knew her girls were in contact. It would probably only make her feel worse.

"Not really, we exchange messages now and again, but not on a regular basis," Julie replied and looked to the bathroom door again.

"Well, Sam is right; Rhonda is an amazing grandmother, and she loves taking care of her grandkids. But she knows you aren't ready to settle down or have your own yet."

Julie smiled. "I always knew she would be a fabulous granny. Mom does love kids. And I'm really glad Sam gave her two because I'm not planning on contributing any."

I cocked my head at her. "How can you be so certain already? You're what, twenty-nine? You still have plenty of time to change your mind."

"I'm thirty-two," Julie corrected. "You didn't have any and you seem pretty happy to me."

My eyebrows knitted together. "It wasn't really a conscious choice; it just didn't happen."

Part of me regretted not having children, but during my most fertile years I was too obsessed with my career as an art history professor to find a boyfriend, let alone raise a family. And by the time I met my husband Carlos, we were both in our late thirties. Sure, we could have had kids and been the kind of parents that often get confused for the grandparents, but it wasn't really on our agenda, at least not at first. And by the time it was, I was deeply in love with my job and knew that sleuthing around the world wouldn't combine well with raising a family.

"Speaking of which, Mom told me what happened. I'm sorry I couldn't get back for Carlos's funeral. Did they ever find the, uh—body?" She whispered the last word so softly it was almost inaudible.

I shook my head, momentarily unable to speak. Grief overwhelmed me at times like these, and I knew it was better to hold my tongue than release a torrent of tears over the poor girl. Carlos's death was still too painful to talk about, and it had left a hole in my heart that I feared could never be repaired.

Luckily, Rhonda returned from the bathroom before we could continue down that path.

"I'm so sorry for that waterfall of emotion, darling, but I just can't believe you're here. It had been so long since I've gotten to hold you." Rhonda threw her arms around her daughter again, but managed to keep her cheeks dry.

This time, Julie hugged her back with the same intensity. "Mom, I am so glad to see you. It's been too long." When she gave her mom a kiss on the cheek, I was certain Rhonda was going to lose it again. But thankfully she kept her emotions in check long enough for us to find our luggage and get out of the airport.

Rhonda didn't let go of Julie's hand until we reached the Residenza Venezia.

When our taxi approached the hotel Cyril had recommended, my bestie leaned over to me. "Would you mind if Julie and I shared a room? We have a lot of catching up to do."

"Of course! I kind of figured you would want some space to talk."

"Thank you, Carmen. You really are a wonderful friend."

I smiled at over at her, but she'd already turned back to her daughter. Yes, I was a good friend, but there was more to it. Not only was it fine for those two to spend quality time together, but it also would allow me to move around the hotel and city without Rhonda taking note of my every step.

22

Oddly Evasive

Once I was up in my room, I decided to text the Bighorns' names to Myrtle, instead of calling. She was an insomniac, but it still felt impolite to call in the middle of the night.

As I lay back on the four-poster bed complete with a canopy, I had to take a moment to admire the furnishings and decorations. In contrast to my hotel room close to the Luxembourg Airport, this was a gorgeous space luxuriously decorated with busy wallpaper, thick velvety curtains, and, as the centerpiece, a gorgeous multitiered Murano glass chandelier that must have cost several thousand dollars. If we had time, I hoped to persuade my travel companions to visit the nearby island and the glassmaking factories Murano was so famous for.

Thoughts of sightseeing with the Bighorns reminded me of my current task. While I typed their names into my phone, part of me wondered how the Texan couple might fit into Cyril's smuggling operation. Of course I knew that it was a big "if" to consider. They didn't appear to be working with Cyril, but were a bit too persistent about getting ahold of that painting to be explained away by a rich person's expectation of instant gratification. Their lack of curiosity about my cover story as a journalist was another red flag, in my book.

There had to be a reason other than impatience, to explain their actions. My mind was racing through a multitude of possibilities, one more sinister than the next, when a ping stopped my train of thoughts. It was my phone alerting me to an incoming message. A cry of disbelief rose up when I saw Myrtle's reply. I read it again, then hit the call button.

"What do you mean, they are clean and to focus on the others?"

"Because the Bighorns are a waste of your time. Trust me on this one," Myrtle said, her voice alert.

"Wait a second—you aren't here, but I am. And I am telling you that they are acting strange. Have you even done a background check on them yet? If you did, you didn't send it to me."

"Why can't you just do what I ask and let them be?"

I was used to Myrtle's flippant attitude, blunt remarks, and liberal use of curse words, but she was rarely evasive. But right now, she was ignoring my question, and her cryptic response set my nerves on edge. Both she and Reggie were being unusually closed about everything concerning this case.

"You pay me to use my brain, not just mindlessly follow orders. So what do you *not* want me to know, Myrtle?"

To my surprise, my company contact sighed heavily, instead of reacting in shocked indignation, as I had expected.

"I'm going to have to kick this up to Reggie. I am certain he'd rather tell you himself."

My mouth dropped open. What was my boss up to? There was very little Reggie didn't share with Myrtle, not only because she was a trusted confidant and stellar employee, but also because she was his mother.

"I think I hear him in the kitchen. Let me ask him to call you back. It'll be just a minute."

Myrtle hung up before I could reply, giving me no chances to question her further. I knew she lived in one wing of Reggie's ridiculously large mansion, but did wonder if she could truly hear anyone in the kitchen, from the privacy of her own rooms. Either way, her reaction was unexpected and had well and truly piqued my interest.

Five minutes later, my phone rang again. I snatched it up. I already knew that my boss really disliked Cyril and had been on his trail for years, but what else had he kept hidden away from me?

"Hi, Carmen." My boss's greeting was quite sleepy. Whatever it was that Reggie had to tell me must have been important if Myrtle woke him up for this. "I've been holding back on you, and shouldn't have. But you have to understand: Cyril has been slipping through our fingers for so long, I felt as if I had no choice."

A chill coursed through my body. My boss was usually the most relaxed person I had ever met. His ominous tone was freaking me out. "Reggie, what did you do?"

"You wanted to know who my informant was. Well, Johnny and Josie Bighorn are the ones who tipped me off."

I leaned back, stunned by the news. So they weren't working with Cyril, after all. Otherwise they wouldn't have brought the artist's illicit activities to my boss's attention.

"I also shared with them the same information Myrtle had gathered about the five paintings, which is why Johnny was pushing so hard to win at least one of the five bids," he added.

Now I was truly in shock. Reggie had made such a big deal about keeping Rhonda in the dark, yet he had gladly shared our intel with the Texans? It made no sense.

"I thought you had a strict no-civilians policy, and that Rhonda was the only exception." I kept my tone as neutral as possible, hoping my boss had a good reason for breaking his own rule.

"Yes, well, they did tip me off about having seen two copies of the same painting at last year's auction."

"So that makes them more trustworthy than Rhonda?"

I could hear Reggie pinching his nose. "No, that's not what I'm saying…"

"And why did you send me to the auction if you'd already arranged for them to bid on the paintings? Sending in two operatives seems unnecessary and a touch crazy." The more I thought about what he'd done, the more useless I felt.

"I guess you can call them my backup plan. I needed to be certain at least one of you would be admitted to the party, and the Bighorns were already on the guest list. And I didn't ask them to gather intel, but only to bid on the paintings. You are the one who helped us figure out which ones were most likely stolen, not them."

"Yes, but Lady Sophie called in all of those favors to get me inside!"

"Yes, to get herself and a plus-one invited. But Cyril is apparently quite picky about who he allows into this annual auction, and I wasn't entirely certain he would permit Rhonda to take Lady Sophie's place, despite what his party planner told you. But once you alerted Myrtle that you were in, I figured it was better to say nothing and hope that either Rhonda or the Bighorns won a bid on at least one of the stolen paintings. I would give anything to examine at least one of his repeats for clues."

The ferocity in his voice did not jibe with his typically Zen attitude towards life. It was as if my boss was obsessed with getting Cyril back for something, which was very un-Reggie-like. Frankly, it made me nervous.

"What exactly did Cyril do to upset you so?"

"He has burned countless museums and private collectors with his forgeries, and he still has not atoned for all of his crimes," my boss stated.

I cleared my throat. "He did spend two years in prison for forging art."

"Yes, but he was only convicted for *some* of his crimes—not all of them. There are still hundreds of his fakes hanging in American museums, and we have no way of knowing which are his and which are genuine. The FBI should have demanded that list of forgeries as part of his release. It is quite frustrating," Reggie sputtered. He was getting so flustered, I was afraid it would take hours of yoga for him to center himself again.

"Reggie, did you miss your morning meditation? Why are you getting so worked up about Cyril? We've had more horrible people in our sights, but you were able to maintain a professional distance."

"It doesn't matter."

"Yes, it does. I deserve to know the full story, especially since you wanted me to fly to Italy to follow this lead," I yelled into the phone, fed up with his stubborn refusal to tell me the whole truth. My boss appeared to be out to get Cyril, and I still didn't know why. Until a sudden thought stopped me in my tracks.

"Reggie, did you buy any of his fakes, thinking they were the genuine article?"

His soft sigh was all the answer I needed.

"How many?"

"What do you mean?"

"Don't play coy with me, Reggie. How many of your purchases do you now believe to be Cyril's forgeries?"

"It's not the amount that matters," he muttered.

We were finally getting to the crux of the matter, but at a snail's pace. Yet by his tone, I could tell he was not going to be too forthcoming. What had gotten into my boss? I had a sinking feeling that puzzling that out was going to be crucial to solving this case. However, I really didn't have to time to ruminate on the possible connections between him and Cyril, as well as sort out how the artist was possibly smuggling artwork.

I pinched my nose, hating that I was about to say aloud a sentence that I never expected to have to utter to my boss. "Reggie, I don't have time for these games. Can you put your mother on the line?"

"No!"

"Well, then you'll have to find yourself another art sleuth to work this case. If you don't respect me enough to tell me everything, then I'm done tracking Cyril."

The line was dead silent for a full minute before Reggie finally replied. "Alright. Have you heard of the Andersen Museum?"

That name rang a bell, albeit a vague one. "In Seattle, right? I think I visited it as a kid on a school trip, but didn't it close years ago?"

"Yes, it did, and it's all my fault." He spoke so softly, I wasn't entirely certain that I'd heard him correctly.

"How did you destroy a museum? That doesn't make sense."

"Yes it does. At least when you know the whole story."

"Okay, so spill it—or find yourself another agent." I was done playing the fool. My husband didn't know that he was walking into a deadly trap, because he didn't have all the intel needed to complete the job safely. I refused to take the same risks.

"Jerri Andersen was a wealthy businesswoman and philanthropist. After she retired, she founded the Andersen Museum for Modern Art, on Capitol Hill. It was a glorious space with a wonderful collection of twentieth-century paintings by American and European painters, and I'd gotten to know Jerri well during the opening parties. When I decided to invest in art, she took me under her wing and taught me everything she knew about auctions, private sales, and investing for the long term."

"So we have her to thank for your wonderful taste in art," I added, hoping to lighten the mood. I'd never heard my boss sound so sad before, and it disturbed me quite a bit.

"Yes, Jerri was a true mentor and friend. Which is why when she ran into financial troubles years later, I tried to repay her kindness by purchasing several pieces she'd had her eye on but couldn't afford. It was a unique collection of modern American masterpieces that had attracted quite a bit of media attention, and I thought that if I bought them and donated them to the museum, attendance would surge again. Jerri was thrilled and grateful, so I went ahead and acquired them for her."

He paused for a moment when his voice faltered, apparently under the emotions of recalling these painful events, before continuing in an even softer voice. "The collection did draw in new visitors, and, at first, everything seemed to be going well. Until a few months later, when Cyril was brought to trial and it became known that the art dealer I had purchased the collection from had been knowingly selling Cyril's forgeries for several years."

"Oh, no." My heart went out to my generous boss. All he'd wanted to do was help out his friend, but it sounded like he'd caused a major crisis, instead.

"So everything I'd purchased became suspect, and my act of kindness backfired—big-time. Jerri removed the forgeries from her collection, but it was too late. The local news had already gotten ahold of the story, and a few gossip hounds on the social scene asserted that she'd knowingly bought the fakes at a low price, just to drum up attendance again. All lies, of course, but attendance quickly plummeted to historically low levels, and Jerri ended up closing the museum and selling off most of her collection soon after."

"I'm so sorry." And I really was. Yet, compared to what I was dealing with right now, I couldn't let myself get too worked up about this.

"I've always wanted to make Cyril pay for destroying Jerri's museum. When the Bighorns told me about their suspicions, I saw my chance to get back at him."

I sighed into the phone. *Great, this assignment is personal, not just professional.* That made things so much more complicated.

"So now do you understand why I'm interested in Cyril?" my boss asked, his voice steadier than it had been a few minutes ago. I could imagine it was the relief of finally being able to tell the entire truth that had set him free, emotionally.

"Yes, I think I do." As frustrating as it was to find out about Reggie's obsession with Cyril so late in the game, I knew no good would come from putting him on the spot about withholding information from me. So I tried to push Reggie's vendetta aside and focus on the case at hand.

"Before I let you go, did you share the intel about the five paintings with anyone else—Serena De Ville, perhaps?"

"No, the Bighorns were the only other operatives that I sent in or shared information with. Though Myrtle did tell Lady Sophie the titles of the five paintings we were interested in, when she called us from the party. We didn't know that she'd released herself from the hospital, until she reached out," Reggie said.

"Well then, based on the way she was acting at the auction, and the fact that she won four of the five bids on the paintings we're tracking, Serena may be working with Cyril. Can you ask Myrtle to prioritize her background check?"

"I'll get her working on that, first thing in the morning."

"Alright. I hope you can get some sleep, Reggie."

I hung up before he could reply, hating that I was still questioning whether he had truly told me everything or whether he might still be holding back on me. He was one of the few people I had trusted implicitly. It was going to take some time to get my head around his betrayal.

23

Forced Into Retirement

It took me a few minutes to fully process Reggie's stunner of a call before I could consider my next move. It wasn't just his history with the Andersen Museum that did my head in. I still couldn't believe that he trusted the Texans more than Rhonda. Then again, they had done nothing to make me suspect that they were working for the Rosewood Agency, so they were clearly much better at keeping secrets than my bestie was.

I knew I should call the Baroness before I checked in with the rest. Hopefully she'd had an enlightening conversation with Cyril Bouve after we'd left, and we could wrap this case up in a jiffy.

I dialed her number, clicking the video on as I did. It took a few rings before she answered, and when she did, she looked incredibly tired. It had only been a few hours since we'd talked, but I was immensely glad that she had not tried to join us. From the looks of it, she needed to sleep more than anything else.

"Hey Baroness, you look beat. Why don't you call me back after you've had a chance to rest? I was just checking in and don't have anything new to report."

"I've rested enough these past two weeks," she huffed. "Besides, now is not the time for a nap. I have information to share with you."

"Oh, yeah? I'm all ears." Her snippy tone caused any empathy I'd conjured up to fly out the window. So I leaned back into the hotel's fluffy couch and kicked my feet up on the coffee table.

"It was fortuitous that he and Manzino talked just before we met for brunch, because they had gotten into an argument and Cyril was still quite worked up about it when he joined me." She paused before adding in a triumphant tone, as if it explained everything, "Cyril has a tremor."

"I'm sorry, but you've lost me already."

"Cyril doesn't want to retire, but he feels as if he has no choice, because the tremor in his right hand is getting worse—and fast. His hand shakes so badly that he cannot paint for more than a few minutes at a time. That is why he was so behind schedule with this year's paintings for the Lost Masterpieces auction. He doubts he will be able to paint at all within a few months and wants to retire before his work noticeably suffers."

"So it's not that he wants to stop, but it's that he can no longer paint. Oh my, that is important intel."

"He's told me that Manzino is pressuring him to continue running the gallery, even if it's in name only. But Cyril refuses and has decided to turn it over to his son as soon as he gets back to Luxembourg."

I considered her words. "I bet Manzino was not pleased to hear that."

"Nico doesn't know yet. Cyril only told me that in confidence this morning."

"That's good to know. But why is it so important to Nico that Cyril continue? I wonder if it has anything to do with the framer's death or the supposed art smuggling ring."

"All I know is that Manzino does not want him to stop. Cyril wouldn't tell me everything, but he mentioned that Nico's thought up some scheme to keep him involved, but he refuses to go along with it. If Manzino keeps pushing him, I think he is going to go to the police."

"Oh, so the threats are serious." I quickly caught her up on what I had overheard Nico and Cyril arguing about at the auction the previous night.

"Nico is quite determined to enact his proposed plan, from what Cyril shared. He thinks that is why Nico had the Bighorns' portrait sent to Trieste—to force Cyril to go to Italy, so that he would have to meet up with their boss," Sophie added.

"Wait—Manzino is the reason Johnny Bighorn's painting is on its way to Trieste? Cyril told Johnny that the free port messed up the paperwork."

"Cyril told me it was Nico."

A shiver went up my spine. *Could their boss be Antonio Corozza?* I wondered, knowing I could not share that thought with the Baroness quite yet. She didn't know that I had recently pickpocketed a mobster's phone, one that had contact information leading to the man who probably killed my husband. "Do you know his boss's name?"

"No, I'm afraid Cyril did not say. Whoever it is, he doesn't seem scared of him, more irritated that he is trying to force this meeting. Cyril said that they've had disagreements in the past and nothing bad had happened."

"Yes, but I bet he wasn't threatening to quit before. That changes the dynamic of the conversation. It wouldn't hurt for Cyril to be a little bit scared, or at least on edge, when they meet."

"I suppose," Sophie said, but she looked more bored with the conversation, than worried for Cyril's safety.

"No, I'm serious. His life may be in danger. It sounds like the mob is involved in this operation, somehow."

"Don't they often have a hand in the larger art thefts and international smuggling rings?" my partner said with such disinterest, I wondered how much medicine she'd taken today.

"I suppose it is not a big surprise, considering how many thefts have ties to criminal organizations. But Interpol is also investigating Cyril, and had sent an agent to the auction. He was also at Harold Moreau's villa and recognized me."

My remark must have finally gotten through to her, for she gasped in response. "Oh no! After the last incident, I'm surprised he didn't expose you to Cyril, just to spite Rosewood!"

My partner had recently mentioned that there had been a few occasions during my three-year retirement in which new agents had unintentionally interfered in investigations Interpol was working on. The worst resulted in an art smuggler escaping a sting operation that they'd set up, thanks to a mistake by a rookie agent working for the Rosewood Agency. Since then, there was a lot of bad blood flowing between the two organizations. For this reason, I wasn't entirely certain mentioning Dave to my partner was such a great idea, but figured if I did not, Myrtle would. And it was better that I told Sophie myself.

"No, but he did call his boss, who somehow talked Reggie into lending me to Interpol for this investigation—without asking me first."

When Sophie's hand flew to her chest, I wanted to hug her through the phone. She did get me, in a way that Rhonda, as a civilian, could not. "As if you are a piece of meat?"

"It's okay. In fact, it may make my own investigation easier. Dave should be able to get me into places I usually don't have the authority to access."

To my great relief, my partner agreed. "Hopefully you can wrap up the case faster, this way. So what is Interpol investigating Cyril for?"

"Dave is hoping to get him on tax evasion, but is open to helping me investigate the art smuggling lead."

"Good, it sounds like he might make a fine temporary partner, after all."

I thought of Dave's strong biceps and pretty blue eyes. "Partnering up with him isn't so bad, but I'll be glad when you are feeling better. We work well together."

I was still doing my best to smooth over any residual hurt feelings as a result of the many blunders Rhonda and I had made during the auction, but I truly meant every word I said.

The Baroness jutted up her chin. "Too right. I look forward to our next assignment."

After we hung up, I spent a few minutes contemplating the intel she had shared, before getting ready for a little sightseeing and dinner. How did the framer's death fit in with Cyril's business, and why was Manzino so keen to keep selling his repeats of stolen art? With a little luck, I would find the answers to both questions here in Venice.

24

Sleeping In

At eight in the morning, voices wafted up the hotel stairs, angry enough to make me rise and crack the door open, in the hopes of discovering what the ruckus was all about. I recognized Johnny's voice straightaway, but he was too far away to understand. So I pulled on my clothes and rushed downstairs, not wanting to miss anything.

Rhonda and Julie must not have heard them, I figured, because their door remained closed. I wasn't surprised that they had slept through the noise; we'd stayed up much later than expected last night. After a long walk through the magical city center, we found a café at the base of the Accademia Bridge and had enjoyed the wonderful local wines, fresh seafood, and fantastic views of the colorful homes and churches lining the Grand Canal, deep into the night.

As I crept down the stairs, the voices because clearer and the words audible. "Where is it? Don't tell me it's already on its way back to Luxembourg."

Johnny Bighorn must have been talking to Cyril about his painting, I realized, but it sounded like something else had gone wrong with the delivery. I slowed my pace and ambled down the last three steps, as if I was simply walking to the breakfast room. The two men were standing close to the reception desk, battling it out with words. Josie stood a few steps behind, as if she wanted no part in their disagreement.

In one of the comfy-looking wingbacks sat Dave, staring at his phone as if he was reading. I would bet money that he was really listening in on the two men's conversation. A tingly sensation coursed through my body as I noted how dashing he looked in that burgundy polo shirt and gray slacks. I resisted a juvenile desire to wave to him, and instead casually sat down in the chair closest to me and pulled out my phone, in the hopes that neither Cyril or Johnny would notice me, either.

"No, it's nothing like that. Manzino must have drank too much last night because he's had a late start. He just called to say he is on his way to the Trieste free port now, and I suspect your painting will be here shortly."

"I've had enough of your excuses. Josie, I think it's time we drive over there and get our painting back." Although he was clearly speaking to his wife, Johnny kept his eyes locked on Cyril.

If I hadn't known that they were working with Reggie, I would have been suspicious of their actions. Yes, rich people did tend to expect that their desires would be fulfilled immediately, but Johnny's tenacity was borderline obsessive. I hoped he wasn't pushing Cyril too hard.

Apparently the artist didn't find Johnny's behavior suspicious, because he folded his hands under his chin, as if he was praying the Texan would actually listen to him. "It doesn't work like that. Only Manzino is authorized to take it out. It'll be here as soon as it can be. It takes time and quite a bit of paperwork to clear customs. Why don't you go sightseeing, and I'll call you as soon as it arrives?"

I noted that Dave's eyebrow shot up, as if something on his phone's screen had surprised him. I didn't think much of it, until he glanced over at me and smiled, as if he was trying to telepathically communicate something to me. Unfortunately, I was not a mind reader, so I stood and stretched, before slowly making my way towards him. Luckily, more of the hotel's guests were coming down for breakfast, so my movements were less noticeable.

Josie laid a hand on her husband's arm. "Johnny, why don't we go pick up our painting after breakfast. I'm famished."

Her face-saving suggestion was apparently just what her husband needed to back down.

"Tell you what, if you still haven't heard from Manzino by the time we are done, I'd like you to give him a call. Alright?" Johnny said, in a more diplomatic tone.

Cyril nodded. "Good idea. There's no sense in rushing off now and missing this delicious-looking buffet."

When the two men slapped each other on the backs and walked amicably towards the dining room, with Josie in tow, I slipped over to Dave and sat across from him. We leaned our heads in towards each other, but before I could utter a word, I heard a familiar voice behind me.

"Pillow talk?"

I looked up to see Rhonda standing with her hands on her hips and a twinkle in her eye. Her daughter was just behind, a silly grin plastered on her face, as well. Lord only knew what stories her mother had told her about my supposed infatuation with Dave.

I rolled my eyes and whispered to Dave, "Give me a minute."

When I rose, so did my voice. "Rhonda, I slept in my room last night—and alone."

"That's too bad. I thought one of us might find a little romance during our European adventure. Although it's not over yet. There's still hope for us," Rhonda said as Julie hooked an arm through her mother's. They both looked radiant. I could only imagine how cathartic it was for them to spend so much quality time together, especially after such a long hiatus.

"Dave and I were discussing our plans for the day. I'll catch up with you in a minute, alright?"

"Sure thing. It better be something romantic, like a gondola ride. That might just be what you two need to get to know each other better." Rhonda winked before sauntering off with her daughter in tow.

I turned back to Dave, pretending Rhonda's interruption hadn't occurred. "So, what's up? From your reaction a minute ago, I'd say you've discovered something interesting."

"You heard Cyril tell Johnny that his painting was still at the free port, right? But according to this tracker, it left Trieste an hour ago and has been sitting in a warehouse in an industrial-looking building close to Venice ever since."

"What do you think is inside it?"

"I don't know yet, but I can ask the local police about it later. First, I want to get a look at the Bighorns' painting. If Cyril is telling the truth, it should be delivered to the hotel today. However, they've been so possessive of it, I doubt the Texans will let us get close to it. So I was thinking we could steal it from their room—and give it back later, of course."

I smirked. "That won't be necessary. In fact, I think it's going to be easier than either one of us suspected."

Dave was quiet a moment. "What do you mean?"

"They are working for Rosewood."

Dave leaned back into his chair. "Wait—what? I didn't think your organization used civilians."

I blushed. "I didn't know about it either until we arrived in Venice, but Johnny was the one who informed my boss about Cyril's possible involvement with the art smuggling ring. Because he already had an invitation, Reggie asked Johnny to bid on the five paintings we suspect are stolen."

"Well, I'll be. I figured a loudmouth like him wouldn't be able to keep quiet about working for Rosewood."

"I was pretty surprised, too," I admitted, omitting my irritation with my boss for not telling me earlier, as well as Rhonda's involvement with the assignment. "They don't know that I know. Do you mind if I tell them?"

Technically we were partners for this operation, which was why I felt obligated to ask.

"Certainly, although I'd like to be there to see their faces when you do."

"Is that a good idea? Then I'll have to explain why Interpol is involved."

"Fair enough." Dave wagged a finger at me. "You promise to tell me everything?"

"Certainly. Speaking of, I would like to have that chat with them now, before the painting arrives. I'm going to see if they are in the breakfast room, alright?"

"Be my guest."

25

The Texans Come Clean

I spotted the Bighorns in the dining area, feasting on a vast selection of pastries and, luckily for me, sitting alone.

"I know why you are here." I kept my expression jovial and my tone light as I slid into a chair across from them.

Both Johnny and Josie paused midbite, their flaky croissants frozen in midair.

"Reginald Rosewood asked you to bid on five specific paintings last night, didn't he? He's my boss and just informed me that you were also working this case."

"Phew, that is a relief." Johnny let his pastry fall to his plate. "Reggie told us that you were one of his agents, but that you didn't know about our involvement."

I had expected more shock or astonishment on their part, but neither seemed to be truly surprised by my revelation. Reggie must have already warned them that I now knew.

"It took all of my willpower not to react, when Rhonda mentioned on the plane that you were a journalist," Josie interjected.

"Especially since we knew it was a lie," Johnny added.

"I have a confession to make," Josie whispered dramatically across the table. "We don't have a daughter named Gertrude. Her real name is Trudy, and she looks nothing like the girl in the portrait. I figured it was a good cover story, to explain why we just had to have it. Reggie did say that money was no object, but to ensure that we won the bid on at least one of the five he had his eye on."

I pursed my lips, put out that I wasn't allowed to tell Rhonda what we were really up to, when Reggie had clearly told them everything.

"Yes, well, I'm glad you did. That will make it easier to examine the painting after it arrives."

"Certainly! We were going to encourage you to come up to our room and check it out, even though you weren't supposed to know why," Josie said as she patted my hand.

"That's good to know," I said, then looked up to find Julie watching us rather intently.

Something about the intensity of her gaze made me nervous, causing me to wave hello, which she then interpreted as an excuse to join us. *Whew, good thing I didn't notice her trying to catch my eye earlier*, I thought.

As she made her way over, I leaned across the table and locked eyes with the Bighorns. "Can we keep this assignment between us? Reggie doesn't want everyone to know that you're helping Rosewood out with this or why I am so interested in the painting, alright?"

"Of course, our lips are sealed," Josie exclaimed, just as mother and daughter approached.

"What's sealed?" Julie asked as she set her plate onto the table.

"Not 'sealed.' 'On sale,'" I explained. "We were talking about a shop we'd noticed last night. They sell the cutest scarves with tiny gondolas embroidered onto them, and Josie thought they were on sale. I might stop by later and get one. They are really adorable."

"I should pick up some souvenirs and gifts, too, and those sound perfect. Maybe we can join you. What do you think, Mom?" The way Julie eyed me as she spoke turned her words into more of a provocation, than an expression of interest in souvenir shopping.

"Sure, that would be great. I only hope we can find it again. The streets here are a maze."

"It won't hurt to try, will it?" Julie replied, but the way she said it, it was pretty clear that she did not believe me. Considering I was lying about the shop and conversation, I couldn't blame her. Julie always had been the smartest of the bunch; I would have to watch what I said around her.

We chitchatted about this and that during breakfast, but there was an underlying sense of tension permeating the meal. The Bighorns were obviously trying to play it cool and remain calm, but by the way Johnny tapped his left foot and Josie played with her sleeve's hem, it was obvious the two did not completely trust Cyril or the Italian art dealer.

Which made Cyril's sudden appearance in the dining area, just as we were finishing the dregs of our coffee and Johnny was threatening to go find him, an enormous relief. The art dealer's grin and the large, flat object in his hands meant good news for the Bighorns.

Cyril crossed over to the couple and bowed slightly. "Your portrait has arrived."

26

The Arrival

"Can you take another picture of us with it? Golly, she's even prettier here than she was in the gallery. It must be the natural light," Josie gushed.

Rhonda, Julie, and I had followed Cyril and the Bighorns up to their hotel suite, so we could admire their painting. Johnny held his newly acquired portrait in his hands, smiling like a proud papa.

"Are you satisfied?" Cyril asked. Apparently he was done being civil, for since the portrait had arrived, he'd acted as if he wanted to get this transaction over with and disappear. By the way he kept checking his watch, I wondered whether he'd already scheduled a flight back to Luxembourg.

Johnny laid his painting gently onto the bed and held out his hand to the artist. "Immensely satisfied. You've outdone yourself, Cyril. It's too bad you're going to hang up your brush."

"Well, they say it's better to go out on a high note, than drag along." He glanced over at the rest of us, making eye contact with me, Julie, Rhonda, and the Bighorns, before nodding once. I was surprised that Julie wanted to tag along, simply because she'd never really shown an interest in art. In fact, I had the feeling that one of her rebellious acts as a youth had been to avoid museums and galleries, in order to pester her art-loving mother.

"If you will excuse me, I have to speak with Manzino before…"

His words were cut off by his ringing telephone. He pulled it out of his pocket and stared at the screen, as if he couldn't believe that the person was calling. "This is Cyril speaking."

His expression darkened, and he put a finger in his free ear. "Serena, slow down. I can barely understand you."

A moment later, a wave of irritation washed over his face. "What do you mean, your housekeeper has had a heart attack? What does that have to do with me?"

Cyril suddenly noticed that we were all listening in. "Give me a moment, Serena; I have find a quieter place to talk."

"Enjoy your time in Venice," he called out as he strode over to the door.

"I wonder what that was all about," Johnny said after he'd left.

"I hope that lady is alright. It sure is sweet of Serena to be so concerned about her help's health," Josie added.

I bit on my lip to suppress the caustic comment on the tip of my tongue. My targets and their associates lived in a different world than I did, a fact that I sometimes had trouble remembering. So I ignored Josie's remark and caught Johnny's eye.

"Say, do you mind if I take a closer look at your portrait? I'm a huge fan of Manet."

"Sure, come on over, Carmen." Johnny waved me closer. When I was standing right next to him, I gazed down at the painting as I whispered, "We have to get rid of Rhonda and Julie. I'm going to waste a little of your champagne—is that alright?"

Johnny's face lit up as he turned to the three other women in the room and slapped his hands together. "Who's up for another glass of bubbly?"

Rhonda giggled like a schoolgirl. "I don't know, the first glass has already gone to my head. And it's not even noon."

"Ah, Mom, live a little," Julie scolded. Yet when Rhonda's head tilted down, she threw her arm around her mother's shoulders and squeezed. "I'm just teasing. We don't have to have another glass if you don't want to."

Rhonda brightened back up. "Of course, you're teasing. And yes we do—we have lots to celebrate. The Bighorns have their painting, and I have you! Another glass would be lovely, Johnny."

The Texan poured more into our glasses, while I examined the canvas's surface with my eyes. I was itching to get my hands on it, but needed my friend and her daughter to exit the room first.

Once my glass was full again, I maneuvered myself closer to Rhonda and Julie, before whipping around, with my glass tilted forward. As I'd hoped, the champagne arched out of my glass and splattered all over Rhonda's dress and Julie's pantsuit.

"Oh, lordy—I just bought this dress!" my bestie exclaimed.

"I'm so sorry, Rhonda! Let me get a napkin."

"Don't! It'll only rub the champagne into the fabric. Shoot, I need to wash this out in a sink, before it settles."

She looked over at the portrait, then down at her dress. "I'm going to go change, but I'll be back in a jiff."

"Take Julie," I whispered.

"Why? I don't need help changing clothes," Rhonda said, a touch too loudly.

I grimaced and glared at the painting until her eyes widened in understanding.

"Julie, darling, could you help me out? The zipper catches on the fabric real easy and it'd be a shame to tear it. Besides, you should wash out your pants, too."

Her daughter looked torn, and by the way she kept her eyes on the painting, it seemed as if she wanted some alone time with the canvas, as well. But why? It was a lovely composition, and the painter had captured the light beautifully, but it wasn't Manet's best work.

"Back in a jiff!" Thankfully, Rhonda grabbed her daughter's arm and pulled her out the door, before she could say no.

As soon as it clicked shut, I ran my fingers across the surface. The thin coating of varnish covering the paint still felt sticky. It usually took a week to harden, meaning it had been applied in the past few days. The underlying layers of oil paint were quite thick and protruded out from the surface. I pushed my fingernail into a blob of paint close to the frame, and it sliced right through it.

"What do you see, Carmen?" Johnny asked.

"It's so strange. Cyril had used quite a bit of paint to make this portrait, but hadn't even waited for the top layer to harden completely before varnishing it."

I turned the painting over and noted that at each of the four corners, the raw canvas had been folded neatly, like a well-wrapped present, before being nailed into place. When I pushed into the fabric, I was not surprised to see that it flexed with my movements. So the canvas underneath the painting was not old, either; otherwise, it would have been stiff from being folded into one place for so many years.

"There is no way this is a canvas that dates back to 1872. The corners would be as hard as a rock by now."

I stood upright and stretched out my back. "This is a new canvas and new painting, bearing Cyril's signature. I would bet money that this is a genuine Bouve repeat, and not the original it was based on."

"Well, that's too bad. After that framer made such a fuss about Cyril moving stolen art around, I thought we might just have hit the jackpot," Johnny sulked.

"Not that we would have kept it, you understand," Josie added with a blush.

"Of course not. And don't you fret—that is one theory shot down, but I still have a few more to test."

I ran my fingers along the back of the frame and around the inner edge, which is how I discovered that Dave's tracker was still in place. The sticker was almost completely transparent, making it almost undetectable, unless you knew what you were looking for.

However, it was no longer parallel to the frame's edge, but had shifted so that a fraction of it stuck out over the edge. Yet when I tugged on it, it stayed in place. Had it gotten so warm during transport that the glue had loosened slightly, causing the sticker to shift, before hardening again? I doubted it, because then the entire painting would show signs of heat stress.

Had the portrait been manhandled to such a degree that the tag had moved? I doubted that, too. Considering how many pieces of fine art were moved through the free ports, I would expect them to be experts in handling such items with great care. Whatever the reason, Dave would be pleased to know the tag was still on the frame, even if it had shifted slightly.

I turned the painting over and pushed down on the canvas, just enough to examine the painted edges under the frame, when something caught my eye as off. So I took another look at the right- and left-hand sides of the painting, letting my thoughts wander until my subconscious pointed out the oddity to me.

I looked to the Bighorns, both silently watching me examine their painting. "The entire canvas is slightly off-center. If you look at the painted strips underneath the frame, I think you'll see what I mean."

I pulled my torso back as far as I could so they could get closer to the work, while still pushing down on the painting's edges ever so slightly.

Johnny made a show of studying it intently, before shaking his head. "I'm sorry, but I don't see it. Do you, Josie?"

When Johnny looked to his wife, she shrugged. "I'm sorry, Carmen, but I don't, either."

"That's alright," I chuckled. "This isn't a test."

I nodded to the right-hand side of the painting. "On the right, the entire strip of canvas under the frame is painted. But if you look at the left-hand side, you'll note that the paint ends just at the edge of the frame, and the rest is a stripe of raw canvas. Because the canvas is typically stretched over the frame before the painter gets to work, usually both edges are covered in paint, not just one."

As I looked at the two sides again, another thought struck. I turned the portrait over and pulled out my phone, before shining the flashlight into the thin space between the canvas and frame. "Now, that's interesting. I can't say for certain without removing the frame, but it looks like there are another set of holes in the canvas, as if it had been nailed onto the stretcher frame once before."

I pointed out the row of holes in the canvas, a few millimeters away from where the staples were currently poking through it.

"I think this painting has been restretched since it's been painted, and that the second framer mucked up and now it's slightly misaligned. Which makes absolutely no sense."

Josie and Johnny looked at me as if I was speaking a foreign language. "I'm afraid you've lost us, Carmen," Johnny finally admitted.

"The canvas is almost always attached to the stretcher frame before the painter starts to work on it. There's no reason to restretch a painting, unless the wood has rotted, but that usually takes decades. And it's not something most framers do willingly, because it is always a challenge to get the edges to line back up perfectly. This portrait is a case in point. So why did it have to be restretched, if Cyril only painted it a few weeks ago?"

Josie and Johnny nodded as if they understood what I meant, but I doubted they did. "What I'm trying to say is that someone took the canvas off of the frame after it had been painted, and then nailed it to a new one. Which is a real pain in the butt and something no artist wants to have happen, unless it is absolutely necessary. You need to be a highly skilled framer to get it right. So why did someone go to all that trouble?"

I looked down at the portrait again, wishing the young girl could whisper the answer to me. Unfortunately, she could not. "It would be prudent of me to take the frame off and check that there is an extra set of holes around the entire canvas, but Rhonda and Julie will be back before I could get all of the screws loose. Maybe I can do that tonight, after you've returned from your sightseeing trip."

"Sure, whatever you need to do. Your boss paid for it, so technically it's the property of the Rosewood Agency," Johnny said.

My thoughts immediately turned to the dead young man who had worked in Cyril's framing department. How I wish he was still alive so that I could interrogate him. He probably had the answers I needed to solve this, which was probably why he had to die, I reckoned. I would have to ask Dave whether there were any new leads into his death.

But a misaligned canvas on its own didn't help me prove that Cyril was smuggling anything, at least not yet. Before I could further reflect on what I'd seen, or what it could mean, a knock on the hotel room door brought my examination to an end.

"Yoo-hoo, it's Rhonda and Julie," my friend called out in a singsong voice.

It was disappointing that I couldn't find anything more obvious, but I had to console myself that I'd only had a few minutes to scrutinize the painting, and only superficially. Perhaps when I relayed my findings to Dave, a new thought would occur to me.

When Josie pulled open the door, Julie rushed inside and over to the painting, with Rhonda lagging behind. "So what's going on?"

"Nothing much. We were talking about taking a long walk around Venice today, instead of joining a tour. You know, let our feet lead the way for a change. There are so many gorgeous churches and incredible squares here; it really is a magical city," Josie enthused.

"Oh, that sounds like a good idea," Julie said, even though she sounded disappointed, not excited about Josie's proposal.

Rhonda snuck up behind me and leaned in so close, I could smell the breath mint she was sucking on. "Speaking of magical, what's going on with you and Dave? I saw you two holding hands at the auction. And did I catch you smooching in the lobby?"

"No, you did not. But if you all don't mind, I would like to spend the day with him. It's been years since I've been on any sort of date, and it might get awkward, especially with four chaperones." I averted my eyes and blushed, in keeping with our ruse that I was interested in him romantically. I hated having to lie, but I really needed to get away from the rest so Dave and I could do some investigating.

"He sure is a good-looking fellow. If I didn't have Johnny here, you'd have some competition for that one," Josie guffawed, as did Rhonda.

Johnny, however, didn't seem to get the joke, because he narrowed his eyes at his wife, as if she was seriously contemplating leaving him.

Josie must have noticed, too, for she wrapped her arms around her husband and squeezed him tight. "You know I would never leave you, Big John. We're soulmates, so you're stuck with me!"

Her husband pushed up the brim of his hat and pulled his wife in for a passionate kiss that had the three of us looking away. When they finally broke free, Josie wiped her mouth with the back of her hand and smiled up at her husband.

"Johnny, let's see about putting this little lady in the hotel's safe. After that, we can do some sightseeing. Why don't we meet up in the lobby in a few minutes?"

"That sounds perfect," Rhonda said as she pulled off her lime-green sweater vest and fanned herself with one hand. "I know I was just there, but I'm going to pop up to my room and change into something lighter. It's already warmer than I expected, and I bet we're going to get hot walking around all day."

"That's a good idea," I said as I looked down at my pants and long-sleeved blouse. There had been a chill in the air this morning, but since the sun had broken through the clouds, the air coming through the open windows had warmed up considerably.

"Alright. We'll see you two down in the lobby in a bit. And Carmen, good luck today." Josie's chortle filled the room as we exited.

27

No Discretion

When I reached my room, Rhonda and Julie stopped in front of my door, instead of continuing down the hallway to reach theirs.

"Can we come inside for a minute?"

I hesitated with my hand on the door handle as I looked over at my bestie. "As long as you aren't going to give me a pep talk about Dave and how perfect we are together, you are welcome to come in."

"No, it's nothing like that, though he is pretty sexy. And he can't seem to keep his eyes off of you," she giggled. Julie was thankfully refraining from teasing me, which pushed my estimation of her up even more.

I knew his interest was just part of our cover, as was that fantastic kiss. Yet would it be so terrible if Dave was interested in me? It had been years since I'd even considered going out with anyone in the romantic sense. In the middle of an investigation was not the time to find out, though. Perhaps, when this was all over, we could get a drink, but until then, our relationship had to remain professional.

As soon as the pair were inside and the door closed, Rhonda asked, "What do you think of the Bighorns' portrait? Did you find any clues as to how Cyril is smuggling the real art into Italy? Or is this truly just one of his repeats?"

I gritted my teeth, wondering why she couldn't keep her mouth shut. Yes, Julie was her daughter, but I had taken Rhonda into my confidence.

Even worse, Julie didn't look shocked by her mom's question, but rather eager for an answer. Just how much had Rhonda told her about my current assignment?

I counted to ten backwards in my mind, refusing to allow my irritation to overrule the logical portion of my brain. I could get mad at them both and demand that they leave my room, but that would only be a short-term solution. Knowing Rhonda, she would keep hounding me about this, and I couldn't risk her saying something inappropriate in front of the other guests. Besides, she had obviously told Julie more than she should have, and right now, I could use all the help I could get.

I shook my head and sighed, knowing Reggie would kill me if he found out that I'd taken Rhonda and Julie into my confidence, yet feeling as if I had no other choice.

Luckily they interpreted my gesture as an outing of my frustration with this case, not them. Especially when I used my fingers to quickly tick off the theories I had already tested.

I paused and chewed on my lip, after relaying almost all that I had discovered so far. "The only odd thing about the Bighorns' portrait is that the entire painting is slightly off-center, as if it had been recently restretched and the framer didn't quite get it right. And it looks like there are a few extra holes on the sides, where staples or nails have already gone through the canvas. However, unless I can take the frame off, I cannot be certain."

Rhonda nodded along, absorbing all I had told them. "That is unusual."

"I really thought he had doubled up the original and his repeat, but the canvas visible on the back is new and unpainted, not old, so there goes that theory. It would have been the easiest way to do it, and the one with the least risk of harming the original. So now I'm at a loss," I admitted with great reluctance.

To my surprise, it was Julie who spoke up next, not Rhonda.

"On my first assignment in Prague, I was asked to assist a young man who'd gotten in trouble with customs when he tried to leave the country. It turned out that he had stolen a page from a medieval manuscript during a tour of a private library—one with an illustration on it—and was trying to smuggle it out of the country."

"That happens more often than you'd think..." I started to explain, but Julie talked over me.

"The man had hidden it inside a hardback book he'd purchased at a local market, by placing the stolen page in between the cover and that sheet of paper glued to the inside of it. Gosh, what is that called again?" Julie's forehead creased as she paused to ponder the term.

"The endpaper," her mother answered.

"That's it! Thanks, Mom. So he'd hidden the illustration between the cover and endpaper, kind of like a sandwich. Ironically, the customs officer thought the book he'd hidden it inside of was a rare manuscript, so they pulled him aside so they could examine it thoroughly. It's a good thing they took their time, too. The customs officer only discovered the stolen page because it was the dead of winter and the radiators were turned up so high that the glue the man had used had melted just enough for the customs officer to notice that the endpaper had come loose. He almost didn't find the stolen page because the cover and endpaper were genuine."

"Like a sandwich," I muttered as the answer I had been searching for struck me like a thunderbolt of lightning. "Rhonda! Do you remember when you knocked on that painting at the auction?"

"Do I ever. Lady Sophie may never speak civilly to me again because of that blunder."

"You said it sounded 'odd.' What did you mean by that?"

"Oh, yes, it sounded duller than I had expected. The canvas is usually stretched quite tight over the frame, otherwise it will ripple once paint is applied to the surface. But it could have been poorly stretched, or a few nails could be loose. Sloppy, sure, but it sounds like Cyril was rushing to get everything hung up in time for the auction."

"Or there is another, more sinister reason. What if it was three layers of canvas nailed together, not one? Like a sandwich," I said with a twinkle in my eye before springing up and bear-hugging Julie.

My startled goddaughter stood frozen, her face a mask of confusion, as I cried, "It's what's in between that matters, not the painting on top or the raw canvas visible on the back. Julie, you are brilliant!"

28

Tiaras and Film Stars

"I've got to tell Dave!" I cried out.

Rhonda gasped as her hand flew to her heart. "Wait, is he a journalist, too?"

Julie dipped her head and seemed to be smirking. I frowned at her, hoping she would give her mom a break. Sure, Rhonda was dramatic, but it was all part of her charm. But now was not the time to chastise Julie.

"No, I guess I got so excited that I suddenly wanted to kiss someone and his name popped into my head." I blushed as my lame excuse poured out of my mouth.

It was Rhonda's turn to wrap me up in a hug. "I'm so happy for you. If I didn't have Julie with me, I would be so jealous right now."

"Don't get too excited about it. I don't know whether Dave and I are going to work out," I said and frowned.

I hated this ruse, but it was a useful way to get away from my friend without upsetting her. I couldn't wait to tell my temporary partner about Julie's sandwich comment. I was certain that was how Cyril was smuggling the real works down to Italy, along with the copies he'd made, but we needed hard evidence if we were going to get any jury to convict him. Which meant we had to figure out where the real and fake canvases were separated from each other. Dave had mentioned that the Bighorns' painting made an unscheduled stop between the free port and hotel. If Cyril or Nico had removed the original before delivering the copy to the Bighorns, it must have happened there.

"Of course you don't! You just met him. I'm simply thrilled that you are opening yourself up to love again."

I rolled my eyes, imagining the juicy conversation Rhonda would be having about me today, with Josie most likely. "Thanks, my dear. Now if you will excuse me, I'm going to call Dave."

I had almost gotten them back out of the door, when my phone rang. Unfortunately, Rhonda saw the screen and who was calling.

"What great timing! I've been wanting to introduce her to Julie. Do you mind?"

She grabbed my phone out of my hand and answered it, before I could react.

"Lady Sophie? This is Rhonda Rhodes. How are you feeling?"

"Oh, Rhonda, how charming. Is Carmen with you?" I heard my partner reply. I knew "charming" was a term she only used when upset or irritated. When Rhonda switched on the video, I understood why. Sophie was sitting up in bed with her tiara in place, but had no makeup on. The bruise on her jaw cast a shadow over part of her face, and the circles under her eyes were a deep blue.

"Yes, I'm here," I called out from over Rhonda's shoulder as I tried to wrestle my phone back from her.

But Rhonda was having none of it. She swatted my hand away, then turned the phone's camera towards her daughter.

"Before I give you to Carmen, there's someone I'd like you to meet. This is my daughter, Julie!"

Sophie's expression remained neutral, but one eyebrow did raise ever so slightly. "Hello, are you enjoying Venice?"

Julie waved into the phone, seemingly unsure what she should say. "Hello, Lady Sophie. Yes, I am so far, thanks."

"Your tiara is simply stunning—isn't it, Julie? I noticed the unusual cut of the diamonds when we met last. I had one on my show a few years ago that Grace Kelly had once worn! Do you know your tiara's history? I know an expert who's helped me out in the past. I can ask her about yours."

I knew Rhonda babbled when she was excited or nervous. I wasn't certain which one it was, but she was talking so fast I could barely understand her. Fortunately, my partner didn't have any trouble following along.

In fact, Sophie's lips un-pursed as she seemed to contemplate Rhonda's question. "No, I don't believe anyone in my family has. It would be lovely to know more about its history, but please don't feel obligated to consult your acquaintance about it."

From the surprisingly genuine tone of Sophie's voice, it appeared that she'd never considered it, but thought it was a good idea.

By the way Rhonda brightened up, I knew she had taken the Baroness's comment to heart. I'd bet money that my bestie would make the time to research Sophie's tiara, if only as a way of showing Sophie that she cared. That was just the kind of person she was.

"Let me take a screenshot." Rhonda took a picture before my partner could cover her face with her hands.

"Please don't share that one on social media, or at least blur out my face. No one can see me like this. I look horrible!"

"Of course, I won't. It's to show that expert, in case our paths cross again."

I knew Rhonda was up to something when she quickly changed the subject by launching into a long retelling of our brief walk around Venice last night, and what she hoped to see today. By the way Rhonda was blathering on, I wasn't certain how long it would be before my partner hung up on her. But to my delight, Sophie didn't seem bored, and had even added a few suggestions of her own, which were gratefully accepted by my friend. Julie stayed out of the conversation, seemingly content to watch her mother and my partner chat.

Yet when I noticed the strain on Sophie's face, I decided it was time to wrap the conversation up.

"Okay ladies, I think Lady Sophie needs to rest, but I have to talk with her first. Could we have a few minutes alone?"

"Oh, sure." Rhonda sprung up. "We'll give you some time alone with your partner."

"Partner?" Julie asked.

"She's not my partner, but she does help get me into parties that I want to attend, for my job as an antiques journalist. Now, if you don't mind," I said far more harshly than necessary as I gestured towards the door.

Rhonda may not have gotten my hint, but Julie did. "See you later," she called out as she pulled her mother into the hallway.

As soon as the door clicked closed, the Baroness's easy grin disappeared. "Why did Rhonda bring her daughter along? Is she daft?" Sophie was aghast, as I'd expected she would be.

"Technically, Rhonda is not working right now; I am. So this is a vacation for her, which is why she invited her daughter to join us. They have a strained relationship, and this trip seems to be helping. And frankly, I'm glad that Julie can keep her distracted today, so I don't have to worry about her wanting to tag along."

Sophie's chin tilted up. "They seemed pretty chummy to me."

"Thanks to the time they are spending together. Sophie, Rhonda may have made a few silly mistakes, but she is a good person. You really do need to give her a chance."

I felt like I was constantly having to defend my friend's behavior to my partner. It didn't seem right. Would Sophie ever accept her? And what did her refusal to do so, say about me? My working-class background was far more similar to Rhonda's, than the Baroness's privileged upbringing.

"You called me, so do you have any news to share?" I asked Sophie, changing the subject.

"No, I just wanted to check in and see if I can help in any way."

I softened my tone when I noted how tired she really was. "You've already done so much. You don't have to do anything but rest, you know."

"I want to contribute, in any way I can."

I shook my head slightly, knowing there was no point in telling her to back down. Lady Sophie was as stubborn as a mule. "Thank you. But for now, there is nothing you can do. I'll let you know if I need your help."

"Excellent. Did you get a chance to examine the Bighorns' painting?" Sophie pressed.

"I did, and their painting is definitely Cyril's repeat. I have another idea as to how he may be moving the genuine pieces around, but I have to see if Dave can help me arrange for a search warrant first, to check my theory."

I wasn't ready to share everything with her, knowing she would relay any new intel to Myrtle and Reggie. I didn't want my boss to get his hopes up quite yet.

"That sounds like a serious lead."

"It could be—or it could be another bust. I'll keep you all posted."

29

Romance in the Air

Dave was still in his room and waiting for my call, which meant we could depart immediately. After agreeing to meet in the lobby, I skipped down the steps, figuring I could ask the receptionist for a lunch recommendation before he joined me.

When I entered, Johnny and Josie were walking out of the hotel's security center and over towards Rhonda and Julie, standing by the front desk.

"Hey, Carmen, I thought you had a date with Dave," Josie called out, causing me to blush.

"We do; he should be down any minute," I replied.

"They're going on a gondola ride. Isn't that romantic?" Rhonda whisper-shouted to Julie, winking at me as she did.

Josie grinned up at her husband. "We should go on one, too."

"You got it, little lady. Anything to make you happy." When Johnny pulled his wife close, Josie melted in his arms. It was adorable to see how much in love the two were.

When Dave entered the lobby moments later, Rhonda waved him over. "Speak of the devil. Hey, Dave, over here."

"Okay, I'll see you all later," I said as I turned to my temporary partner, but Rhonda held me back, instead.

"No, wait, I want to introduce him to Julie first."

"Is that necessary?" Our fake relationship certainly didn't warrant introducing him to my goddaughter. I hated that I was lying about being romantically interested in him, and hoped that Rhonda didn't expect us to cuddle or hold hands.

"It'll just take a minute, then we will leave you two lovebirds alone."

When Dave joined us, Julie was making a point of searching through her tiny purse for something and didn't look up until Rhonda cleared her throat.

"Julie, this is Dave, Carmen's friend."

The way she said it, implied so much more. I blushed fire-engine red as Dave laid an arm over my shoulders. "I haven't seen Carmen in weeks, not since that party in France. It's been fun catching up."

His wolfish grin implied things that were not true, making me jerk out of his embrace.

The two shook hands, but Julie seemed to avoid eye contact. By the way she was acting, I would venture to guess that they had once been romantically involved, and she was doing her best to be civil in our presence. But how would they know each other? Maybe Dave was based out of Prague. I'd have to ask him about that later.

Johnny pushed up the brim of his hat. "Well, ladies, what do you say we head out?"

"Are you sure you don't want to join us?" Josie asked me.

Dave pulled me in close, as Johnny had his wife, and kissed the top of my head. "If you don't mind, I'd like Carmen all to myself today."

Josie's eyes and smile widened as she nodded her approval. "That sounds mighty nice. You two have fun now, you hear? I know we're going to have a grand time!"

"I can't wait. Thanks for inviting us to tag along," Julie enthused, patting Johnny amicably on the arm.

Josie apparently didn't appreciate the much younger and prettier woman making physical contact with her man, for she grabbed onto her husband's arm and pulled him close again. "Yes, well, we are looking forward to seeing more of this romantic city together."

The mention of romance seemed to have reminded Josie of our supposedly budding one, for she turned her attention back to us fake lovebirds.

Standing here with Josie grinning at me and winking at Dave, I felt obligated to add, "We'll catch up with you later tonight, alright?"

The Texan eyed Dave, her grin widening the longer she looked him up and down. "More than alright. I expect a full report, tonight or tomorrow—depending on what you two get up to tonight."

"Oh, my," I muttered under my breath as I felt my cheeks reddening. When Rhonda started making kissy faces at us, I grabbed Dave's hand and pulled him towards the door, before he caught sight of my bestie, doing her best to embarrass me.

30

Catching Dave Up

When Dave held the hotel door open for me, the sights, sounds, and scents of Venice raced in. I could almost taste the freshly caught fish being delivered to the restaurant's kitchen downstairs, see and hear the many clock towers ringing in the noon hour, and feel the drips of water whipping off of the boats racing down the canal.

"I'm famished. Do you want to walk and talk, or would you rather sit down somewhere? I have a lot to catch you up on," I said, as soon as we were outside.

"I say we sit down and enjoy the meal. After you've filled me in, we can plan our next move."

"Fair enough." As much as I wanted to tell him about my sandwich theory straightaway, he didn't have all of the intel that I had. I thought it only fair to share everything I'd learned this morning in the Bighorns' room, so that he could draw his own conclusions, as well.

So we found a cute little café with plants hanging from every rafter and hook, and canal-side seating. I ordered a salad topped with fresh seafood, and my taste buds were soon thanking me for it. Everything in the dish—from the ripe tomatoes to the gigantic olives and crispy calamari rings—tasted as if it had just been plucked from someone's garden or fished out of the sea. It was heavenly.

Between bites, I got Dave up to speed on what I had seen this morning, which admittedly wasn't much.

"Well, that's disappointing. Maybe Cyril isn't moving stolen art around, after all," he muttered into his pastrami sandwich, slathered in truffle mayonnaise.

"Hang on—I have another idea, one I formed thanks to Rhonda's daughter," I said, excited to share my latest theory.

"You mean Julie? What did she say?" By the way Dave cocked his head as his brow shot up, I figured he must not think much of Rhonda's daughter.

"Her story isn't important, but the idea it inspired is. What if Cyril had put the original painting in between two other canvases?" I pointed to his sandwich. "The two new canvases are the slices of bread, and the original is the meat in the middle. That would explain why the back appears to be new—because it is!"

Dave leaned back and stared at the meal in his hand, temporarily awestruck. "Like a sandwich."

"Exactly. It's so simple that it is ingenious."

"Oh, that's good. No, that's brilliant! But how are we going to test your theory?"

"You said that the Bighorns' painting made a stop, before arriving at the hotel. Have you found out more about that address?"

"Yes, the local police helped me out with that one. It's a warehouse in an industrial district that Manzino's been leasing for the past eight years. He uses it as a restoration studio and storage facility for his gallery in the Dorsoduro Sestiere district of Venice."

"It's Manzino's storage facility? That makes perfect sense—we know that Manzino and Cyril are working together. And isn't his gallery close to the Peggy Guggenheim Museum? That neighborhood sounds familiar."

"It is. You have a great memory."

"Not really. It was my favorite stop when my husband and I visited Venice years ago."

I smiled as I recalled walking hand in hand with my beloved Carlos when we visited the Guggenheim collection. I couldn't recall much about the art we saw, but I remembered every detail of what my husband wore that day and how he had smiled down at me, with so much love in his heart and eyes.

"I'm sorry about your husband. I read about it in your file," Dave said.

His words caused my visions of my Carlos to vanish. "Sure you did." I took a large gulp of my hibiscus tea. "Have you asked about a warrant to search the premises yet?"

"I did, but the local authorities are dragging their feet on it. And Manzino stores millions of dollars' worth of art inside of the facility, which means we really cannot enter without one."

"Do you think the local cops are moving slowly intentionally, to prevent you from getting inside? Or is it simply a matter of bureaucracy at its finest?" I knew Interpol agents had to coordinate with local law enforcement agencies, because they didn't have the proper jurisdiction to act, otherwise.

Dave smirked. "I'm not sure what to think yet. It's only been a few hours since I put the request in, and it is a Sunday. Italy is a pretty religious country. It could simply be that the judge who has to approve it is still at church."

"Alright." My suspicious nature meant that I was less inclined to believe it was a matter of an official's church attendance, but then again, I hadn't had much contact with Italian law enforcement because I hadn't worked many cases in this country.

"Until we get permission to go inside, we could go and take a look at it, from the outside, I mean," I said, grasping at straws. I doubted we could solve this case without getting inside of Manzino's warehouse and hoped I could persuade Dave to bend the rules just a little, once were standing outside the building. I knew he needed everything to be on the up and up if he was to convict someone. But right now, I was more interested in gathering intel than bringing Manzino in.

Dave smiled as he touched his napkin to his lips. "You know, I was thinking the same thing. We don't need a search warrant to look through the windows. Fancy a ride?"

A smile slowly spread over my face. "Yes, I do."

He signaled for the check, and as we waited, a thought popped into my head. "Oh, before we go, something strange happened at the hotel before we left. Cyril received a cryptic call from Serena, telling him that her housekeeper had a heart attack. Do you know what that's all about? I'm surprised someone like Serena cares about her staff, frankly."

Dave chuckled. "I doubt she does. No, what Serena probably meant was that the Italian police who broke down her front door almost gave her housekeeper a heart attack."

His words caused me to freeze. "What are you talking about?"

"After you told me that the Bighorns were working with the Rosewood Agency, I figured I would try to get ahold of the four paintings Serena bid on, so we could examine them, as well. Apparently my Italian counterparts were a little too enthusiastic."

"What did they do?"

"I probably shouldn't laugh, but the housekeeper didn't respond to the bell, and the police outside heard strange noises, so they busted the door down. Apparently the poor woman was deep-cleaning a rug with a noisy machine and had headphones on, so she hadn't heard the bell. But she sure did notice when the cops stormed in!"

I crossed my arms over my torso to keep my sides from splitting. "Sorry, I know I shouldn't laugh either, but I would have given anything to have seen that." When I got my breath back, I added, "What did they find out?"

"Their art division's experts examined all four and found nothing suspicious. They are exactly what the customs forms say—Cyril's repeats." He blew out his cheeks. "So that's a bust, too."

"Wait a second, that's actually good news. It supports my sandwich theory. Serena's four paintings made the same stopover as the Bighorns' portrait, before they were delivered to her house, right?"

"Yep. We really do need to get inside of that warehouse." I recognized that glint in his eye. It was the same one I got when I had my target squarely in my crosshairs.

31

Guns Blazing

As soon as a taxi dropped us off a few blocks from Manzino's warehouse, Dave began calling all of his local law enforcement contacts, in the hope of hearing that the search warrant had been approved.

Unfortunately, it was turning into a bureaucratic nightmare. I still wasn't sure whether the locals were intentionally dragging their feet to protect the art dealer, but things were moving molasses slow.

While he called, I peeked inside every window I could reach, but the building was larger than I had expected, and I couldn't access a large section of it, from the outside.

I could see a plethora of crates stacked up in one room and several paintings resting on easels in another, but the sheets covering the canvases made it impossible to work out what they were paintings of.

Another room appeared to be filled with cleaning supplies and nothing nefarious. But the most promising space was a sparsely decorated room containing a few filing cabinets, a computer, and a large desk that could have come from IKEA. *That must be Manzino's office*, I figured. I looked down from my position on the dumpster, to see Dave still pacing as he spoke rapid Italian with his local counterpart. My grasp of the language was too weak to follow it completely, but I could tell that the warrant still had not been approved.

He hung up and ran a hand through his hair, before stepping back towards me. "Still a no-go, and I'm out of contacts to call. Which means there's nothing left to do but wait for the judge to get back to us. I suppose we could keep an eye on the place until we hear back. If Manzino does move any art out of here, then we could at least tail him."

I kicked at a rotting banana peel hanging off of the edge of the container, flinging it into the air. "You know as well as I do that we need to get inside."

"This isn't a movie; we can't just barge in with guns blazing. Besides, anything we find will be inadmissible in court."

"Right now, all I want to do is gather intel. If we can confirm that Manzino and Cyril are actually sandwiching the original in between two canvases, then Rosewood will find another way to get to them," I pressed.

"But wouldn't it be easier to wait? Then I get to arrest the bad guy, and you can search his office."

"Sure, if we get a warrant before Manzino moves the paintings. Otherwise, I'm out of luck. I bet the originals are under those sheets, although there are only three, so far as I can see from here. He might have already moved one. How much longer are you willing to wait?"

When he didn't answer, I cupped my hands against the window, wondering again what was resting on those easels. "So where do you think the originals are headed?"

"I bet they will be whisked off to another storage unit or used to pay off a debt. But I doubt they'll surface again anytime soon."

"Which means we can't let these paintings go. If we walk away now, that's four more stolen paintings gone forever," I argued.

"Yes, but is recovering them worth harm coming to us? Because that is what will happen if anyone finds us inside of that warehouse. Without a warrant, we wouldn't be able to call for backup, either."

"Come on, Dave, live a little. The Rosewood Agency has been after Cyril for years. You heard him announce his retirement at the auction. This is probably going to be his last shipment. If we don't get him now, we may never be able to hold Cyril accountable for his part in this smuggling ring."

I looked up and down the alleyway, which ran along the back of the building. Since we'd arrived, ten minutes earlier, not a single human soul had wandered by. However, several rodents were scurrying about, and the longer we hung around, the more they seemed to be getting interested in us. Kicking the overripe banana peel to the ground hadn't helped matters.

"Look, this is the kind of place that in films, the mob uses to kill off thieving extras. I say we either break in or pack up. My vote is for the former."

Dave gazed up at the building, obviously contemplating his options, before finally saying, "Let's do it."

"That's the spirit!" I hopped off of the dumpster and skipped over to the front door.

"Wait—we better put these on." He rummaged around in his jacket until he found two pairs of rubber gloves, then handed me one.

I donned the gloves, then rushed up to the front door, my trusty bobby pin in hand. I always traveled with a few tucked into my thick hair. They were the perfect way to pick a lock, especially since my boss frowned on me carrying around anything that could be construed as criminal, such as a set of lockpicking tools. Or at least, it usually was. However, this lock was electronic.

"Shoot. We'll have to pry open a window."

"No, we won't." Dave stepped forward with the same electronic gizmo he'd used to open the gallery door in Luxembourg. He must have noticed me gazing at it enviously, because he held it in front of me and grinned. "Would you like to give it a whirl?"

"Would I ever!"

Dave showed me which buttons to push, and a few seconds later, the door popped open.

"I really need one of those," I muttered as I followed him inside, knowing my boss would never allow me to carry one around.

The space was dark and creepy, but we didn't dare turn on the overhead lights. Instead, we used our phones as flashlights to illuminate a path. We tiptoed our way past a climate-controlled storage room and a supply closet, before reaching a rather large restoration studio. At the back of that was Cyril's office.

Part of me wanted to tear his desk and cabinets apart in search of clues to the identity of his criminal associates, but more of me wanted to see whether my theory about the painting sandwich was correct.

I beelined my way over to the three easels in the center of the space, all covered with a white sheet, presumably to keep them dust free. I carefully pulled off the first, revealing the landscape by Cezanne—one of the repeats Serena De Ville had purchased. However, this was not Cyril's version. The paint had a luminosity only gained through age. Most telling were the creases on the corners of the frame. They were as hard as a rock.

Bingo, I just found me an original. I repeated the process twice more, revealing a real Canaletto and Matisse, giggling in delight as I took in our discovery.

"We've got him, Dave. These three paintings are the genuine versions of the repeats Serena De Ville purchased. I wonder where the fourth is."

Close to the easels was an open trash can. I poked my hand inside and pulled out an untreated canvas, with Cyril's signature on one side, and holes around the edges, where the nails had gone through.

"There are a whole bunch of these in the trash. They must have been attached to the back of the smuggling sandwich," I sang out, giddy with excitement.

"Check it out—I bet this is the fourth painting," Dave cried as he removed the lid of a wooden crate, resting on the opposite side of the room. When he pulled a bubble-wrapped object out, I could feel a surge of excitement coursing through my veins. After he'd removed the packaging and held up the painting, I smiled in recognition. It was the fourth painting Serena had purchased, a rugged landscape by Casper David Friedrich. But this was the real deal, not one of Cyril's copies.

"Cyril has been a naughty boy," I said, a smile in my voice. This was my favorite part of the job—finding the evidence needed to put away the bad guys. Now all we had to do was get the police to come down here and search the premises. From what we'd found so far, they should have enough evidence to arrest both Cyril and Nico.

"Manzino's not much cleaner, either." Dave smiled. "It's time to call this in."

A few moments later, he had his boss on the line. "We cracked the case. We have found enough evidence to tie both Bouve and Manzino to the smuggling charges, and maybe even to a forgery one, too. I bet we'll find paperwork to support my tax evasion theory, as well. But we need that warrant to make it official."

As Dave listened, the creases in his forehead deepened. "But one was already crated up for transport. I don't know how much longer we can—"

Dave's boss must have cut him off. His mouth flapped closed, and the longer he listened, the darker his expression grew. Moments later, he muttered, "Yes, sir. I understand."

He sighed deeply after hanging up, then turned to me, his head already shaking "no."

"What did he say?"

"We need to get back outside, and under no circumstances are we to re-enter the building or remove anything from the premises. He's going to pressure the locals to get that warrant sorted out, but that's all he can do for us. My boss is right that we don't want to damage the chain of evidence. That's how scumbags get free—on technicalities."

I nodded, despite my deep desire to ransack Manzino's office, anyway. "He has a point. We should go."

32

To Kill or Not To Kill

As we set about putting everything back exactly as it had been when we arrived, I couldn't help but exclaim, "We just rolled up an international smuggling ring. I'm feeling pretty good about all of this. How about you?"

"I'll feel better once we have that warrant. But we were able to figure out what Cyril was up to, thanks to our international cooperation." He looked over and smiled at me, in more than a professional way.

"Yes, well, we solved the first mystery, in any case. We still don't know who killed the framer, Enrico."

That stopped Dave in his tracks. "Why does it matter who killed him?"

"Enrico was obviously telling the truth about what Cyril was doing. And he was threatening to blackmail Cyril or expose him to the cops if he didn't pay him to stay quiet. So Cyril must have killed the framer, to shut him up—permanently. I doubt Bighorn did it to keep his reputation clean."

"I don't know." Dave frowned. "Killing the framer is pretty extreme. Besides, his murder is not our concern. We'll pass our intel on to the local police and let them deal with it."

"If they aren't in Manzino's pocket, you mean. He must have been operating here under the radar for years. Do you really think they are going to thoroughly investigate Cyril, especially if Manzino is involved?"

Dave sighed. "Not every Italian takes a bribe or is associated with the mob."

"Of course not, but your own intel suggests that Manzino is very much involved with the local mafia. They are probably protecting him and anyone he's working with. I bet that's why we still don't have a warrant."

"Then I'll pass our intel on to another division of Interpol."

I froze as another thought struck. "Maybe Enrico knew about Nico's involvement, as well. He may have also tried to blackmail Manzino, after the auction was over. Which would give him just as much reason to kill Enrico as Cyril."

I pointed towards the office, only a few feet away. "Dave, all of Nico's paperwork is right there. We might find something incriminating, like a threatening note or a blackmail letter."

He sprung in front of my extended arm, as if to block me. "No! We do this the proper way, to ensure the criminal pays, which means we wait until the Italians come through with that search warrant. I'm not going to let Rosewood mess up this assignment, as well."

I rocked back on my heels. "Oh, so that is what this is really about. Sophie told me about a new agent messing up a sting operation a few years back. But I'm no rookie."

"Carmen, you know as well as I do that even if we find something incriminating, we won't be able to use it to convict either man of the crime, not if we don't have the proper authority to be searching his office in the first place. Heck, we don't even have the right to be in here right now. Which means I need to get outside and persuade my Italian colleagues to get us that warrant."

He gestured towards the front entrance. "Shall we?"

I looked longingly at the office door, only a few steps away. But Dave was right. It was better to let this investigation happen through the proper channels, if we wanted to convict Manzino and Cyril of art smuggling. The murder would have to be dealt with later.

33

Murderer on the Loose

It was obvious from Dave's tone and expression that his mind was made up. I knew Reggie would be furious with me if I messed up our cooperation with Interpol, so I stepped through the restoration studio door and into the hallway without another word.

We were a few steps away from the entrance, when we heard voices outside the building, close to the front door.

"Could that be the security guards?" I whispered.

"I don't think so—they are speaking in English. And they sound pretty ticked off."

I listened to their voices, trying to place them. "Shoot—it's Cyril and Nico, and they are coming inside! Quick, we have to hide. Come on!"

I grabbed Dave's hand and pulled him back through to the restoration studio just as someone began punching numbers into the keypad. When we reached the darkened space, I shone my phone's flashlight around, searching for a good hiding place. I quickly settled on a long table across from Manzino's office and crouched down behind it, in the hopes the two men would end up there. They were my main suspects in the framer's murder, and with a little luck, their argument would shed some light as to which of them did it.

When Dave squatted down beside me, his sweet-smelling cologne filled my nostrils. I didn't know what fragrance he was wearing, but my body was reacting to it—and his close proximity—in a primal way. It took all of my willpower not to deeply inhale his delicious scent, or rub my face across the slight stubble on his chin. But we were partners, not lovers, despite that fantastic kiss. So I kept it professional.

"Five bucks says Cyril did it," I whispered, careful not to lean in too closely, for fear of getting lost in his scent again.

Dave's eyes widened in response. "You bet on this kind of thing?"

I shrugged. "Sure, why not?"

Dave cocked his head for a moment, studying me, then shrugged back. "Okay, I've got ten on Manzino. There's something fishy about that guy."

"And not about Cyril?"

He leaned in so close, I could feel the warmth of his breath. "You make a good point. Still, I'm sticking with my gut feeling."

"Fair enough." I turned my attention back to our pair of suspects, already walking through the restoration studio and rapidly approaching Manzino's office.

We didn't have to wait long to settle the bet.

"I still don't understand why you had to kill Enrico," Cyril muttered as the office lit up, presumably from Nico switching on the overhead lights.

When Dave looked to me and smirked, I pretended to be devastated, but really I was just glad to know who had killed the young man.

"You left me no choice. You should have picked your crew for the auction more carefully," Manzino replied.

"You sent Enrico up to me—I figured he was trustworthy."

"Apparently we were both wrong because Enrico came to my hotel room and threatened to tell the police everything about our operation if I didn't pay him a substantial amount."

"The nerve of that guy. He must have decided to try you, after I ejected him from the party. Still we could have paid him off," Cyril said, so softly, I could barely understand him.

"And risk our boss finding out about it?" Nico laughed. "No, he had to be silenced. That's why I lured him away from the hotel and bashed his head in with a rock. The arrogant man never saw it coming."

"What does our boss care?"

"Are you joking—who do you think we work for? He would never have allowed you to be blackmailed for this, but would have had you killed, instead. And what if Enrico had gone to the police in Luxembourg? I'm protected in Italy, but not up north. With him gone, our problem is solved. You should be thanking me."

"For taking another human's life—are you crazy?"

"No, for cleaning up your mess."

"I didn't sign up for murder. This is exactly why I'm retiring," Cyril stated, his tone resolute.

"About that—our boss wants to keep everything going, as is. It would be easier if you signed the paintings, but if you refuse, we'll have Cyprus do it."

"Leave him out of this! He doesn't know what I've been doing for you, and I know he would never approve."

"That is disappointing. Our boss made it pretty clear to me that if you don't play along, Cyprus will take your place. Otherwise, he's a dead man. It's his choice."

"This is a nightmare!" Cyril cried.

"He can make his 'inspired by' paintings, as long as he continues with the annual Lost Masterpieces auction. That's all we ask. Considering how much younger he is, I expect he could paint fifty copies a year, instead of twenty. Who knows, our bosses might be happy you want to step aside."

"No! I refuse to go along with your scheme or to let our boss get his claws into Cyprus. If you continue to threaten me, I am going to go to the police and tell them everything. I don't care what happens to me, but Cyprus stays clean."

I was touched that Cyril would do anything to keep his son out of the Mafia's hands, but knew he had just signed his own death warrant by sharing that thought with Manzino.

Apparently, the Italian agreed. "You shouldn't have said that. Our boss will never let you walk away from this now. And I'm not going to let you drag me down with you, either!"

A loud clanging noise made Dave and I freeze, but Cyril's scream of terror a moment later had us both springing up from behind the table to see Manzino chasing the artist around his desk with a framer's hammer.

When Nico swung with surprising accuracy and bashed one of Cyril's wrists with the tool, the painter's scream tore through my soul.

"My hand!"

Cyril was apparently in so much pain that he didn't notice Nico winding back to hit him again. But we did.

Dave shot over the table and launched himself at Manzino, startling the Italian before he could get a good swing in. His feet connected with Nico's torso, knocking the dealer onto the ground. Yet when Dave's body kept moving forward and he landed on the other side of Nico, the Italian swung wildly, hitting Dave right on the temple, knocking him out cold.

"Dave!"

I felt a surge of anger rise up inside of me when I saw Manzino pulling back to swing again. So I grabbed a metal ruler, the heaviest thing within reach, and flung it at Nico's chest, as if it was a ninja's throwing star.

It didn't pierce his skin, but it did knock the wind out of him and cause his hammer-wielding arm to fall back to the ground. Before he could get back up, I was on top of him, my knees pushing down onto his elbows with my full body weight, so that he couldn't get another shot in at either one of us.

Manzino squirmed under my weight, until I managed to wrangle the hammer out of his hand.

"If you try anything, I'm bashing your temple in." I raised the tool up over my head and glared at him with as menacing of an expression as I could muster. My threat was enough to make him stop wiggling.

"Dave? Are you alright?" I cried, wondering how hard Nico had hit my colleague.

"I think so," he replied groggily. When he ran a hand over his forehead and pushed back his blood-soaked hair, I could see a nasty wound. Thankfully, the blood had already stopped streaming out of it.

"And Cyril—how are you doing?"

The artist held his wrist tight as he crouched next to Manzino's desk and glared at the Italian art dealer, from a safe distance. "I'll live, thanks to you and Dave. What a horrid mess. Cyprus must never know what I've done."

I couldn't help but laugh. "I seriously doubt you'll be able to keep this news from him. Heck, soon the whole world will know what you and Manzino have done."

I could feel Manzino's body go limp, presumably as he began to grasp the gravity of his predicament.

Dave patted Cyril on the back. "Carmen is right; you are about to be breaking news."

The old artist put his hands over his face and wept.

34

Police Station Espresso

I sipped the coffee in my hand, savoring the delicious blend and perfectly steamed milk. It was the first time I'd had great coffee in a police station. I had to hand it to the Italians and their love of espresso.

Through the two-way mirror in front of me, I could see a pair of investigators interviewing Nico Manzino. A small speaker mounted on the wall provided the audio. Dave had arranged for me to listen in on the police interrogations of both Nico and Cyril, even finding an officer to translate for me on the fly. My father might have been Italian, but I never really learned the language. His family's desire to take me away from my mother had made her less inclined to celebrate that side of my heritage.

Dave, the translator, and I sat next to each other on one side of the room, while a cluster of Italian detectives discussed the interview in their native language, on the other side.

To our great relief, Manzino confessed to everything. At least, once the police agreed to get his wife and five children into the witness protection program. After that, he sang like a bird.

It did help that the Luxembourg cops investigating Enrico's death had found Nico's fingerprint in the blood on the rock used to kill Enrico. Unbeknownst to us, by the time the interview started, there was already a warrant out for Manzino's arrest.

Yet Nico was obviously more worried about what the mob would do to him than either of the police forces. Throughout the interview, he maintained that the criminal organization he worked for would have killed his family, if he refused to cooperate. Apparently it was shortly after he began to represent Cyril that a local gangster approached Nico with a deal he couldn't refuse. All he had to do was recruit Bouve to work on his scheme. Once Nico waved a bunch of cash in front of the forger, Cyril readily agreed.

It turned out that Cyril's talents were exactly what a local mafia figure needed to make his plan a reality. Since artwork was often used among criminals as a form of payment, Nico's boss decided to have Cyril forge copies of artwork his crew had stolen, so that he would have two ways of paying off a debt, instead of just one.

The originals were sent to Cyril's gallery in Luxembourg throughout the year, usually shortly after they had been stolen by one of the organization's many operatives. After he was finished copying it, the original was sandwiched in between Cyril's reproduction and a blank canvas. It was then shipped from the Luxembourg to the free port in Trieste, where Manzino had it transported to his warehouse. There the sandwich was taken apart. The blank canvas was discarded, and Cyril's copy and the original were reframed.

One version was stored in a secured, climate-controlled vault, for future use. The other was sent on per his boss's orders, typically to pay off a debt or serve as a down payment for a large drug transaction.

The auction was a way of justifying the many shipments Cyril made to Nico's gallery and helped to provide a cover story for how the artwork had entered Italy. Which was why Manzino was so keen to keep everything going as is. It was crucial that either Cyril or Cyprus continue to make exact copies of the artwork, not just paintings in the style of.

The cherry on top was hearing that Cyril was, in fact, still making forgeries. Nico explained how Cyril often shipped other works to him through the free port, fakes he'd signed with the original artist's signature, before adding a layer of varnish and his own on top of it. After those pieces made their way through customs in Italy, it only took a little turpentine and a steady hand to remove Cyril Bouve's name, transforming his "repeat" into a forged masterpiece capable of fooling the mob.

Nico's story put a smile on my face. While I had been chasing after an art smuggling network, and Dave for signs of tax evasion, the reality—that one criminal organization was trying to cheat several others—turned out to be far more devious. Instead of a museum falling victim to Cyril's forgeries, they were meant to shortchange a gangster. It was brilliant.

Yet as open as he had been about what he and Cyril had done, Nico was quite reluctant to tell the police who he was actually working for. I kept hoping that he would name Antonio Corozza, but when he finally did reveal which suspicious character he was working for, it turned out to be the wrong mob boss. He answered to Pietro Denaro, a northern Italian criminal long sought by the local authorities. The Italians were thrilled, but all I could do was sigh.

After the police took a weeping Nico back to his holding cell, it was Cyril's turn. He was just as forthcoming, because as he stated right from the get-go, he hoped to avoid a long prison sentence by telling the police everything.

Which was why he was so willing to explain in great detail how the entire operation worked—who his criminal contacts were, which paintings he had copied, and how he moved both his versions and the originals around Europe. The details about how the stolen paintings had been shipped to his gallery was a gold mine of information for the international law enforcement community.

From the way he described it, making these forgeries from stolen artwork was one big adventure that he'd enjoyed taking part in, and if his hand hadn't given out, he would have gladly continued. I couldn't blame him. The mob paid him handsomely to keep his mouth shut, and he got to do what he loved most. For Cyril, it had been a win-win situation.

I was feeling pretty good about life when Dave and I walked out of the Venice police station. We'd rolled up the smuggling ring, Dave had accumulated enough proof of tax evasion, and Cyril was on record for his part in all of the crimes. I knew my boss would rejoice when he heard the news.

35

A Sunny Day in Venice

Saint Mark's Basilica glistened in the sun, its golden-tiled mosaics and many spires lighting up its glorious exterior. Rising majestically beside it was Saint Mark's Tower, a stately red-brick structure topped with a white marble bell tower and pyramidal spire, upon which sat a golden weather vane in the form of the archangel Gabriel.

I blinked in the bright sunlight, adjusting my eyes so they were focused on the Procuratie before me. The repetitive arches and patterns covering its façade were soothing, especially in this chaotic square filled with screaming tourists and pooping pigeons.

Rhonda and Julie were taking pictures of each other with the many birds circling the square, laughing as they held out breadcrumbs to encourage the pigeons to land on their outstretched arms. I shivered, thinking of all the diseases those flying rats spread. Yet despite the city's many measures to try to chase the population away, there seemed to be no getting rid of them.

It had been wonderful to see so much of the city today, but I was pretty pooped from all the shopping that Rhonda insisted we do. My bestie might be a clotheshorse who enjoyed trying on hundreds of outfits before finally buying one, but I regarded fitting rooms as torture chambers and willingly entered as few as possible.

I took a long sip of my Campari and soda, enjoying the views and the fact that I'd wrapped up this assignment with more ease than expected, when my phone rang.

It was my partner, the Baroness. It was wonderful to see that the color was finally returning to her cheeks. Bed rest had certainly helped, as did my message about us having wrapped up the assignment, I suspected.

"I'm pleased my information about Cyril helped to break open the case."

I knew from Sophie's tone what she was implying, but I was having none of it.

"Yes, it certainly did, and I am grateful for your help, especially in light of your current condition. But before you get too cocky, without Rhonda having knocked on that painting, and Julie telling me that story about the art sandwich, I probably wouldn't have solved the case so quickly."

"Hm" was her terse reply. "It was still unprofessional of Rhonda to have involved her daughter."

"Well, it's a good thing Julie did show up. And as far as her professionalism goes, Rhonda isn't an agent for Rosewood, as you are."

"And it's a good thing she is not. Rhonda does have a heart of gold, but even you must admit that discretion is not her strong suit. Is she agent material? I think not."

So we were finally getting to the crux of the matter. "I have to agree."

Sophie's eyebrow raised.

"Rhonda is not the right person for certain kinds of assignments, such as the Luxembourg auction—I will give you that. But not everyone who steals art travels in the same high-class circles that you do. There are plenty of thieves—like Hollywood director Alistair McPhee—for whom Rhonda would be better suited."

By the way Sophie pursed her lips, I knew she did not agree, but didn't want to argue about it. So I moved on, not wanting to further escalate this pointless discussion. The only person who could make that decision was our boss, Reggie.

"Speaking of which, the next assignment is at Princess Alexandria's castle. I hope you will be feeling well enough to join me on that one. Not only because Rhonda is not a good fit, but also because I know the princess is a good friend of yours."

"Yes, she is; thank you for recognizing that." She looked to her foot, raised up in a sling, high above the bed she was resting in. "Staying in bed has helped tremendously, and the princess's party isn't for another two weeks. If I'm good and keep my foot elevated, I should be able to attend. And from what I recall, she installed ramps and an elevator a few years ago, when her elderly mother came to live with her."

I smiled into the camera. "Then it's settled. We're a team again, Baroness."

A tiny smile cracked her lips. "That's lovely."

When I noticed Rhonda gesturing to Julie and then pointing to our table, I pushed my face close to the screen and rushed my words. "Say, before Rhonda and Julie join us, did Myrtle tell you that Cyril had been making forgeries for the mob?"

The Baroness looked away from the camera, and I swore I saw her blink away a tear.

"Reggie did. I'm still having trouble accepting it, but it sounds as if Cyril had no other choice but to say yes."

I had to bite my lip to prevent myself from saying something nasty. From the way Cyril had described it to the police, it sounded like a fun adventure, until his hand started to give out. What version of the truth did Reggie tell her? No matter, as long as she now knew that her friend was not the person she thought he was.

Perhaps this news would also help to temper her feelings about Rhonda. She had acted as if Cyril was better than people like my bestie, when in fact he was nothing more than a petty criminal willingly working for the mob.

When Rhonda skipped over to our table with Julie in tow, she waved into the camera. "Lady Sophie, it sure is good to see you. The color's come back to your face."

"Thank you; that is kind of you to say. I am sorry that I won't be able to see you again in person before you leave Europe, but do want you to know how happy I am that you could fill in for me."

Rhonda winked into the camera lens. "You aren't getting rid of me just yet! My producer is flying over next week to scout locations. If all goes well, we are going to tape a few shows in Europe."

"That is exciting news," Sophie said. Her voice was quite restrained, but she did appear to be genuinely pleased for my friend. In addition to the news about Cyril, the fact that I had already made clear that I wanted to partner with her—and not Rhonda—for the next assignment probably also helped her to mellow her attitude towards my bestie.

"Wow, Mom, that's great!" Julie hugged her tight.

I patted her on the back, after her daughter had released her from her warm embrace. "That is wonderful news. I'd love to sit in the audience, if that's alright?"

"More than alright! I'd be pleased as punch if you did show up. I'll see about getting you a VIP seat," Rhonda gushed. "My producer is already talking about shooting at least three episodes over here, with the first taking place in Amsterdam."

Rhonda grabbed her daughter's hand. "Don't you worry about coming over to the Netherlands. I don't want you to get in trouble with your boss. I'll see if we can film a show in Prague, too. That way you won't have to take time off work again."

Julie shifted uncomfortably in her seat, causing Rhonda's eyes to cast downward and her voice to break. "Oh, if you don't want me to come over…"

Julie laughed off her remark. "It's not that. I'm just not looking forward to going back to work, that's all. But it pays the bills so I have no choice. Just give me a few days' notice, and I'll make time to be with you."

Rhonda grabbed her hand and looked as if she was going to start weeping again. "Oh, my sweet baby girl—I'm so glad you are back in my life!"

36

Meeting Esmerelda

Julie's flight to Prague departed in a few hours, so after giving her a huge hug, I left her and her mom to spend their remaining time together, and went off in search of Dave.

I found him sitting on a couch down in the lobby, reading a newspaper and apparently waiting for me to show up. He patted the empty space next to him. "Thanks for coming to Italy to help out with the investigation. My boss's opinion of the Rosewood Agency has shot up, thanks to you."

I plunked down next to him, perhaps closer than necessary. "You're welcome, but I was in fact here on assignment for Rosewood, not Interpol."

"Right, you make a good point." When he grabbed my hand and held it tight, it didn't feel wrong.

"So would you like to have that gondola ride now?" I dared to ask.

When he squirmed, instead of looking pleased, my stomach sank.

He squeezed my hand before releasing it. "Ah, yes, I would love to. But I have to deliver a painting first. Do you mind waiting a little longer?"

I pulled back. "Wait a second—that wasn't a lie? There really is an old lady?"

Dave chuckled. "Yes, Dottoressa Bianci definitely exists."

"Huh." I took a minute to digest his news. I thought he'd just made up a great cover story.

"She knows I work for Interpol, but not why I wanted her invitation. She once commissioned Cyril to reproduce a portrait that had been taken from her family during the Second World War. Ever since, she receives invitations to the Lost Masterpieces auctions. She usually doesn't go, which made it easier to take her place."

"Who is she exactly?"

"Dottoressa Bianci owns several palazzos in the city and a few vineyards and estates in Tuscany. Her family is one of the oldest in Venice and has amassed an enormous amount of wealth over the years. She's quite a fascinating woman. Say, why don't you come with me? I'm sure she won't mind. In fact, she'll probably enjoy the company. She is pushing ninety and doesn't get out of the house much. And after we've delivered her painting, we can take that gondola ride together."

I smiled slowly. "Sure, why not? I'm free for the afternoon."

He locked eyes with me. "Great, I'm looking forward to spending more time with you."

His coy words and impish grin made my heart race. I hadn't felt anything for a man since Carlos died. Yet, everything about Dave made my skin tingle in welcome anticipation. Was I finally ready to love again? Maybe crossing paths with Dave was a sign from the universe, telling me that I was.

We grabbed a taxi boat and sailed the Grand Canal to Bianci's regal home, a palazzo as long as a city block and surrounded by an unexpectedly peaceful garden, despite being in the heart of a busy neighborhood. Dave hadn't been lying about her family's wealth.

We were greeted by an elderly housemaid, who took us through to the living room, where a regal old lady sat straight up in a delicately carved, eighteenth-century Venetian rococo armchair, easily worth ten grand.

I swear when I walked through the door, her eyes widened in surprise, but I figured it was my unexpected presence that caused that reaction. Apparently she was too much of a lady to say anything about it.

After a few minutes of mindless chitchat about travel and weather, the Dottoressa tapped her cane on the floor. "I don't know where my maid's manners are. She should have brought in the tea by now. David, would you be a dear and go check on her for me?"

"Certainly, Dottoressa."

As soon as he left the room, the elderly lady turned to me and studied my face so intently, it made me feel as if she suspected me of a crime. After what felt like an hour but was probably a few seconds, I asked, "Do we know each other?"

She leaned forward and ran a wrinkled hand across my cheek, in response. "You remind me of someone I lost long ago. But that's impossible, unless fate brought you to me."

She kept her examination up, so I studied her face, as well, wondering whether her advanced age had perhaps messed with her memories. There was no way I had ever met this woman; of that I was certain. Yet her eyes were crystal clear, and her mind, based on her and Dave's short conversation, seemed to be intact.

So I figured I'd humor her a bit longer and let her study me. Until she suddenly leaned forward and grabbed my wrist with such force, I feared she might actually break it. "What is your full name?"

The intensity of her glare made me answer without hesitation. "Carmen Esmerelda De Luca."

She gasped and crossed herself, before falling back into her chair and clutching at her chest.

Great, I just killed Dave's client, I thought. And for what? I didn't know this lady from Adam. "I'll get help!"

Yet before I could sprint away, she grabbed my wrist again with her claw of a hand and clamped down tight. "No! I have to give you something."

"Are you kidding me? You need a doctor!" I cried, hoping Dave or the maid would hear me. The Dottoressa didn't respond, but instead dug around in her purse, until she pulled out a wallet stuffed so full of photos that the clasp could not latch. Her increasingly labored breaths as she rummaged through them didn't set my mind at ease about her medical condition.

Just as I decided to go get help, she pulled one picture out and held it up to my face. From the angle, I couldn't see what it was of.

"I shouldn't tell you this, but I don't have much time left, so he can't hurt me anymore. Even with these old eyes, I would recognize my favorite nephew's face anywhere."

My stomach dropped, as an eerie feeling overtook me.

"Your what?" I whispered.

When she handed me the photo and I took in the image, my heart just about stopped. It was a picture I knew quite well: one of my father and my mother at Rialto Beach on the coast of Washington state, taken when she was seven months pregnant. I knew that for a fact, because a copy of the same photo had been resting on my grandmother's mantlepiece for decades.

"Why do you have a picture of my parents in your purse?" I felt light-headed. This couldn't be happening. This old lady couldn't have known my parents—could she?

"That is one of my dearest possessions. It is the last photo he sent me. You should have it now."

She grabbed my hand again, but her grip was gentle and warm this time around, as was her smile. "Your father loved you so much. That is why he's dead. He tried to get Antonio's permission to leave, but he wouldn't allow it. I always regret that Carmino didn't listen to me—he should have just disappeared, instead."

My knees gave way as my vision darkened. "Carmino—do you mean my dad? Who is Antonio?" She couldn't mean Corozza; that would be the worst coincidence of all. No, Antonio was a common name. My father was not involved with the Mafia. He couldn't have been.

The woman's words swirled around my brain as I tried to make sense of it all, until my mind couldn't take it anymore and blackness overtook me.

37

Interagency Cooperation

"Carmen, are you alright?" When I opened one eyelid a smidgen, the first thing I saw was Dave, holding one of my hands gently in his. The worry on his face was touching.

"What happened?" I muttered as I dared to open both eyes and looked to my other hand clutched tightly around something. It was the photograph the old lady had given me.

I bolted upright, immediately regretting it. A lump had formed on the back of my head. So I looked slowly to the left, then the right, taking in my surroundings. I was stretched out on a chaise lounge, in the same room, but the old lady was gone.

Dave gently pushed me back down into a more horizontal position. "Hey, take it easy. You passed out."

"Where did Dottoressa Bianci go?"

Dave leaned back on his haunches and looked at me with such concern in his eyes, it made me blush. "She left for a doctor's appointment right after you fainted. I was in the kitchen when it happened. It looks like you nicked your head on the edge of that coffee table when you went down. What happened exactly? The Dottoressa just said that you had suddenly paled and then passed out."

I must have passed out from the shock of hearing that stranger whisper my father's name, I realized. "Can you get in touch with her? I need to see her again."

Dave's expression morphed from concern to confusion. I didn't blame him. Up until an hour ago, the Dottoressa Bianci was a total stranger to me. But I wasn't ready to tell him why I was so interested in speaking to a woman I had just met.

"Sure, I can call her. But she left you this."

He held out a small envelope with my name neatly printed on the front. I ripped it out of his hands and tore it open. Inside was a single sheet of paper. I held the notepad-sized page close to my face so Dave couldn't read along. The message was short and sweet. Well, maybe not sweet, but definitely direct.

"Leave Italy and never return. No good will come from you being here. Do not try and contact me again—your life will be in danger if you do. Know that your father loved you with all of his heart and gave his life to save you. Don't make his sacrifice count for nothing. Your great-aunt, Dottoressa Esmerelda Bianci."

I began to tremble so badly, the paper shook.

Dave's eyes shot open. "Are you sure you are feeling alright? We really should get you to the hospital and have you checked out."

"No, I'm fine," I lied. Did I really just meet my great-aunt, or was it wishful thinking on an old lady's part? But how would she had gotten ahold of that photo, otherwise?

I tucked the picture and letter into my purse, not ready to share either with anyone just yet. Even though he followed it with his eyes, Dave was too much of a gentleman to ask what Bianci had written to me.

I stood up, a tad bit wobbly at first, and used the back of the chaise lounge to keep myself steady. "Why don't we get out of here? You still owe me a gondola ride, and they are pretty pricey, so I'm not going to let you slide on that one."

Dave grinned as he held out his arm. "Sure. Maybe afterwards I can take you to dinner? Call it an investment in our future interagency cooperation."

I raised an eyebrow at him. "Is that an order?"

"No, the assignment is over and now we're simply two colleagues. Dinner will be on me, not the agency."

I snuck a glance at Dave. Here was this good-looking and good-hearted man standing right in front of me, one who clearly wanted to get to know me better. Carlos had been gone for three years, and he wasn't coming back. I didn't know whether Dave and I were destined to fall in love, but it wouldn't hurt to open myself up to the possibility. I was only fifty-two years old and had a long life ahead of me. Perhaps it was time to share it with someone special again, even if that special someone was not Carlos.

I looked over at Dave, wondering whether he would be man enough to take my late husband's place. I couldn't say for certain just yet, but I was finally willing to find out.

So I hooked my arm in his. "Yes, I would like that very much."

Dave pulled me close and lightly pecked my cheek with his soft lips. It didn't feel wrong. In fact, it felt pretty right. And for now, that was all that mattered.

THE END

Thanks for reading *Forgeries and Fatalities*!

Reviews really do help readers decide whether they want to take a chance on a new author. If you enjoyed this story, please consider posting a review on BookBub, on Goodreads, or with your favorite retailer. I appreciate it!
Jennifer S. Alderson

I hope you will join Carmen De Luca for her next mission in *A Killer Inheritance.*
When Carmen's good friend Rhonda Rhodes decides to tape an episode of *Antiques Time* in the Netherlands, she doesn't anticipate discovering a treasure lost during World War II–live on television. Nor did the killer, who will do anything to recover what they see as theirs...

Acknowledgements

I am indebted to my editor, Sadye Scott-Hainchek of The Fussy Librarian, for her outstanding work and advice. The cover designer for this series and my Travel Can Be Murder Cozy Mysteries, Elizabeth Mackey, continues to amaze me with her gorgeous and fun designs.

Many thanks to my wonderful family for helping me create time to write, as well as for encouraging me to keep developing these new characters. I am so grateful for their love and support.

About the Author

Jennifer S. Alderson was born in San Francisco, grew up in Seattle, and currently lives in Amsterdam. After traveling extensively around Asia, Oceania, and Central America, she lived in Darwin, Australia, before settling in the Netherlands.

Jennifer's love of travel, art, and culture inspires her award-winning Zelda Richardson Mystery series, her Travel Can Be Murder Cozy Mysteries, and her Carmen De Luca Art Sleuth Mysteries. Her background in journalism, multimedia development, and art history enriches her novels.

When not writing, she can be found perusing a museum, biking around Amsterdam, or enjoying a coffee along the canal while planning her next research trip.

For more information about the author and her upcoming novels, please visit Jennifer's website [jennifersalderson.com], where you can also sign up for her newsletter to receive updates on future releases, as well as two FREE short eBook stories: *A Book To Die For* (cozy mystery) and *Holiday Gone Wrong* (mystery thriller).

Books by Jennifer S. Alderson:

Carmen De Luca Art Sleuth Mysteries
Collecting Can Be Murder
A Statue To Die For
Forgeries and Fatalities
A Killer Inheritance

Travel Can Be Murder Cozy Mysteries

Death on the Danube: A New Year's Murder in Budapest
Death by Baguette: A Valentine's Day Murder in Paris
Death by Windmill: A Mother's Day Murder in Amsterdam
Death by Bagpipes: A Summer Murder in Edinburgh
Death by Fountain: A Christmas Murder in Rome
Death by Leprechaun: A Saint Patrick's Day Murder in Dublin
Death by Flamenco: An Easter Murder in Seville
Death by Gondola: A Springtime Murder in Venice
Death by Puffin: A Bachelorette Party Murder in Reykjavik

Zelda Richardson Art Mysteries

The Lover's Portrait: An Art Mystery
Rituals of the Dead: An Artifact Mystery
Marked for Revenge: An Art Heist Thriller
The Vermeer Deception: An Art Mystery

Standalone Travel Thriller

Down and Out in Kathmandu: A Backpacker Mystery

Death on the Danube: A New Year's Murder in Budapest

Book One of the Travel Can Be Murder Cozy Mystery series

Who knew a New Year's trip to Budapest could be so deadly? The tour must go on—even with a killer in their midst…

Recent divorcee Lana Hansen needs a break. Her luck has run sour for going on a decade, ever since she got fired from her favorite job as an investigative reporter. When her fresh start in Seattle doesn't work out as planned, Lana ends up unemployed and penniless on Christmas Eve.

Dotty Thompson, her landlord and the owner of Wanderlust Tours, is also in a tight spot after one of her tour guides ends up in the hospital, leaving her a guide short on Christmas Day.

When Dotty offers her a job leading the tour group through Budapest, Hungary, Lana jumps at the chance. It's the perfect way to ring in the new year and pay her rent!

What starts off as the adventure of a lifetime quickly turns into a nightmare when Carl, her fellow tour guide, is found floating in the Danube River. Was it murder or accidental death? Suspects abound when Lana discovers almost everyone on the tour had a bone to pick with Carl.

But Dotty insists the tour must go on, so Lana finds herself trapped with nine murder suspects. When another guest turns up dead, Lana has to figure out who the killer is before she too ends up floating in the Danube.

Excerpt from *Death on the Danube*

Chapter One: A Trip to Budapest

December 26—Seattle, Washington

"You want me to go where, Dotty? And do what?" Lana Hansen had trouble keeping the incredulity out of her voice. She was thrilled, as always, by her landlord's unwavering support and encouragement. But now Lana was beginning to wonder whether Dotty Thompson was becoming mentally unhinged.

"To escort a tour group in Budapest, Hungary. It'll be easy enough for a woman of your many talents."

Lana snorted with laughter. *Ha! What talents?* she thought. Her resume was indeed long: disgraced investigative journalist, injured magician's assistant, former kayaking guide, and now part-time yoga instructor—emphasis on "part-time."

"You'll get to celebrate New Year's while earning a paycheck and enjoying a free trip abroad, to boot. You've been moaning for months about wanting a fresh start. Well, this is as fresh as it gets!" Dotty exclaimed, causing her Christmas-bell earrings to jangle. She was wrapped up in a rainbow-colored bathrobe, a hairnet covering the curlers she set every morning. They were standing inside her living room, Lana still wearing her woolen navy jacket and rain boots. Behind Dotty's ample frame, Lana could see the many decorations and streamers she'd helped to hang up for the Christmas bash last night. Lana was certain that if Dotty's dogs hadn't woken her up, her landlord would have slept the day away.

"Working as one of your tour guides wasn't exactly what I had in mind, Dotty."

"I wouldn't ask you if I had any other choice." Dotty's tone switched from flippant to pleading. "Yesterday one of the guides and two guests crashed into each other while skibobbing outside of Prague, and all are hospitalized. Thank goodness none are in critical condition. But the rest of the group is leaving for Budapest in the morning, and Carl can't do it on his own. He's just not client-friendly enough to pull it off. And I need those five-star reviews,

Lana."

Dotty was not only a property manager, she was also the owner of several successful small businesses. Lana knew Wanderlust Tours was Dotty's favorite and that she would do anything to ensure its continued success. Lana also knew that the tour company was suffering from the increased competition from online booking sites and was having trouble building its audience and generating traffic to its social media accounts. But asking Lana to fill in as a guide seemed desperate, even for Dotty, and even if it was the day after Christmas. Lana shook her head slowly. "I don't know. I'm not qualified to—"

Dotty grabbed one of Lana's hands and squeezed. "Qualified, shmalified. I didn't have any tour guide credentials when I started this company fifteen years ago, and that hasn't made a bit of difference. You enjoy leading those kayaking tours, right? This is the same thing, but for a while longer."

The older lady glanced down at the plastic cards in her other hand, shaking her head. "Besides, you know I love you like a daughter, but I can't accept these gift cards in lieu of rent. If you do this for me, you don't have to pay me back for the past two months' rent. I am offering you the chance of a lifetime. What have you got to lose?"

* * *

If you are enjoying the book, why not pick up your copy now and keep reading? Available as paperback, large print edition, eBook, and in Kindle Unlimited.

The Lover's Portrait: An Art Mystery

Book One in the Zelda Richardson Art Mystery Series

"*The Lover's Portrait* is a well-written mystery with engaging characters and a lot of heart. The perfect novel for those who love art and mysteries!" – Reader's Favorite, 5-star medal

"Well worth reading for what the main character discovers—not just about the portrait mentioned in the title, but also the sobering dangers of Amsterdam during World War II." – IndieReader

A portrait holds the key to recovering a cache of looted artwork, secreted away during World War II, in this captivating historical art thriller set in the 1940s and present-day Amsterdam.

When a Dutch art dealer hides the stock from his gallery—rather than turn it over to his Nazi blackmailer—he pays with his life, leaving a treasure trove of modern masterpieces buried somewhere in Amsterdam, presumably lost forever. That is, until American art history student Zelda Richardson sticks her nose in.

After studying for a year in the Netherlands, Zelda scores an internship at the prestigious Amsterdam Historical Museum, where she works on an exhibition of paintings and sculptures once stolen by the Nazis, lying unclaimed in Dutch museum depots almost seventy years later. When two women claim the same painting, the portrait of a young girl entitled *Irises*, Zelda is tasked with investigating the painting's history and soon finds evidence that one of the two women must be lying about her past. Before she can figure out which one it is and why, Zelda learns about the Dutch art dealer's concealed collection. And that *Irises* is the key to finding it all.

Her discoveries make her a target of someone willing to steal—and even kill—to find the missing paintings. As the list of suspects grows, Zelda realizes she has to track down the lost collection and unmask a killer if she wants to survive.

Excerpt from *The Lover's Portrait*
Chapter 1: Two More Crates

June 26, 1942

Just two more crates, then our work is finally done, Arjan reminded himself as he bent down to grasp the thick twine handles, his back muscles already yelping in protest. Drops of sweat were burning his eyes, blurring his vision. "You can do this," he said softly, heaving the heavy oak box upwards with an audible grunt.

Philip nodded once, then did the same. Together they lugged their loads across the moonlit room, down the metal stairs, and into the cool subterranean space below. After hoisting the last two crates onto a stack close to the ladder, Arjan smiled in satisfaction, slapping Philip on the back as he regarded their work. One hundred and fifty-two crates holding his most treasured objects, and those of so many of his friends, were finally safe. Relief briefly overcame the panic and dread he'd been feeling for longer than he could remember. Preparing the space and artwork had taken more time than he'd hoped it would, but they'd done it. Now he could leave Amsterdam knowing he'd stayed true to his word. Arjan glanced over at Philip, glad he'd trusted him. He stretched out a hand towards the older man. "They fit perfectly."

Philip answered with a hasty handshake and a tight smile before nodding towards the ladder. "Shall we?"

He is right, Arjan thought, *there is still so much to do.* They climbed back up into the small shed and closed the heavy metal lid, careful to cushion its fall.

They didn't want to give the neighbors an excuse to call the Gestapo. Not when they were so close to being finished.

Philip picked up a shovel and scooped sand onto the floor, letting Arjan rake it out evenly before adding more. When the sand was an inch deep, they shifted the first layer of heavy cement tiles into place, careful to fit them snug up against each other.

As they heaved and pushed, Arjan allowed himself to think about the future for the first time in weeks. Hiding the artwork was only the first step; he still had a long way to go before he could stop looking over his shoulder. First, back to his place to collect their suitcases. Then, a short walk to Central Station where second-class train tickets to Venlo were waiting. Finally, a taxi ride to the Belgian border where his contact would provide him with falsified travel documents and a chauffeur-driven Mercedes-Benz. The five Rembrandt etchings in his suitcase would guarantee safe passage to Switzerland. From Geneva he should be able to make his way through the demilitarized zone to Lyon, then down to Marseilles. All he had to do was keep a few steps ahead of Oswald Drechsler.

Just thinking about the hawk-nosed Nazi made him work faster. So far he'd been able to clear out his house and storage spaces without Drechsler noticing. Their last load, the canvases stowed in his gallery, was the riskiest, but he'd had no choice. His friends trusted him—no, counted on him—to keep their treasures safe. He couldn't let them down now. Not after all he'd done wrong.

* * *

If you are enjoying what you are reading, why not pick up your copy now and keep reading? Available as eBook, audiobook, and paperback.

www.ingramcontent.com/pod-product-compliance
Lightning Source LLC
LaVergne TN
LVHW041706070526
838199LV00045B/1229